"There are so many things to love about this book: the characters, the suspense, the courage and compassion of the protagonists, and the fact that kids won't be able to put the book down. At a time when young people feel growing anxiety about the problems in the world, Claude and Medea demonstrate the power of making a difference, and their strange substitute teacher demonstrates the power of education to ignite both learning and action. And who doesn't love a great story about dogs!?"—**Marc Bekoff**, Professor Emeritus of Ecology and Evolutionary Biology at the University of Colorado, Guggenheim Fellow, and author of dozens of books about dogs and other animals

"*Claude & Medea* is a book that matters. A riveting story of adventure and activism, it will engage young people's imagination and also challenge them to think, feel, and, quite possibly, act in some profoundly new ways. It is a must-read for middle schoolers and for anyone of any age who wants to increase their curiosity, compassion, and moral courage. I truly believe this book belongs in school and classroom libraries everywhere!"—**Steve Cochrane**, former Superintendent of the Year, Princeton Public Schools

"Inspiring for young readers and adults alike, *Claude & Medea* tells the story of two New York City teens and improbable friends who learn firsthand what it means to be *solutionaries*—like revolutionaries only "with the goal of solving problems and making a difference." This fictional book takes one on an enthralling city adventure that will surely capture the attention of children while teaching them about environmental, social, and animal issues, such as modern-day slavery and animal research, with both accuracy and sensitivity. Claude and Medea are the kind of hero protagonists our world needs now: compassionate, curious, and courageous. I highly recommend this unique book for school libraries, youth organizations, and any young person in your life."—**Elizabeth O. Crawford**, teacher educator and mom of a nine-year-old budding solutionary

"*Claude & Medea* is a call-to-action and invitation to the table for middle schoolers, educators, and classrooms around the world. From age-appropriate conversations about systemic imbalances, responsible consumption and production, and how to be a force for positive change, the adventures of the Solutionary Squad inside these pages, as inspired by their teacher Ms. Flora Rattlebee, take learning, changemaking, and action to a new level. Imagine if every middle school inspired kids to flip their thinking, choose their own learning adventure, and make the world their classroom!"—**Julia Fliss**, Language Arts, Leadership, and World Studies Teacher

"*Claude & Medea* is an impressive story that will take readers on a journey of self-discovery. Through each character, readers will be inspired to think about how they can impact the world. Teeming with thought-provoking themes such as kindness, preservation, and the humane treatment of all living beings, *Claude & Medea* will remind each of us that when

we endeavor to better the world, we also better ourselves."
—**Andrea Jamison**, Professor of School Librarianship, and former Chair of the American Library Association's Ethnic & Multicultural Information Exchange Roundtable

"*Claude & Medea: The Hellburn Dogs* was the most inspiring book I have ever read. My favorite part was Chapter 6 when Ms. Rattlebee took them on the wonder walk. It's incredible how Ms. Rattlebee opened their eyes to the world by just inviting them to notice all the wonders around them, which inspired them to solve problems that in the beginning, they wouldn't even have noticed. That was my favorite part—how one moment can change you forever. It inspired me sooooo much!"—**Clemence Laigle**, 6th grade student, Evergreen Middle School

"I love seeing a story that shows children can make a difference in the world. The young people that make their way into global media can seem distant and impossible to match. That's where fiction comes in, and Zoe Weil has provided a pair of heroes that everyone can relate to. And which kid hero doesn't want a Ms. Rattlebee?"—**Matt Langdon**, Founder of the Hero Round Table

"*Claude & Medea: The Hellburn Dogs* is a thrilling and engaging read. The story follows the journey of two friends, Claude and Medea, who meet a substitute teacher named Ms. Rattlebee. This encounter leads them to become more aware of the injustices towards animals, and they decide to take action. . . . It teaches valuable lessons about compassion, empathy, and activism. I highly recommend this book to other children and young adults as it is a well-written story that is both entertaining and educational."—**Vienna Langdon**, age thirteen

"A substitute teacher strikes like lightning, jolting some kids out of their middle school trance of self-concern into a sense of wonder, compassion, and determination to seek justice. The kids, led by the passion of Claude and Medea, discover they can create lives of meaning by seeking to do good and defeat corruption. A fun book with a deep message about the need for a generation of solutionaries. Highly recommended."—**Robert Shetterly**, Founder of Americans Who Tell the Truth and author of *Portraits of Earth Justice: Americans Who Tell the Truth*

"Illuminating! Seeing the world through the eyes of author Zoe Weil is always an adventure. In *Claude & Madea*, she delivers a page-turning, first-class detective story, transporting us back to our childhood while delivering a powerful truth: we are all capable of creating solutions to what seem like insurmountable problems. This story reminds us that when we live with compassion toward others, we are given insight that activates our brains to become solutionary thinkers. Every school should have a solutionary squad, and every kid should read this book!"—**Jennifer Skiff**, Author of *The Divinity of Dogs* and *Rescuing Ladybugs: Inspirational Encounters with Animals That Changed the World*

CLAUDE
&
MEDEA

The Hellburn Dogs

Second Edition

Moonbeam Gold Medal winner

Zoe Weil

Lantern Publishing & Media ● Woodstock & Brooklyn, NY

2023
Lantern Publishing & Media
PO Box 1350
Woodstock, NY 12498
www.lanternpm.org

Printed in the United States of America

Library of Congress Cataloging-in-Publication Data

Names: Weil, Zoe, author.
Title: Claude & Medea : the Hellburn dogs / Zoe Weil.
Other titles: Claude and Medea
Description: Woodstock, NY : Lantern Publishing & Media, 2023. | Audience:
      Grades 4-6.
Identifiers: LCCN 2022048377 (print) | LCCN 2022048378 (ebook) | ISBN
      9781590567036 (paperback) | ISBN 9781590567043 (epub)
Subjects: CYAC: Conduct of life—Fiction. | Substitute teachers—Fiction.
      | Dogs—Fiction. | Schools—Fiction. | New York (N.Y.)—Fiction. |
      Mystery and detective stories. | BISAC: JUVENILE FICTION / Animals
      / General | EDUCATION / Schools / Levels / Elementary | LCGFT:
      Detective and mystery fiction. | Novels.
Classification: LCC PZ7.W43335 Cl 2023 (print) | LCC PZ7.W43335 (ebook)
      | DDC [Fic]—dc23
LC record available at https://lccn.loc.gov/2022048377
LC ebook record available at https://lccn.loc.gov/2022048378

Chapter 1

On a brisk September morning, Claude Maxwell-Cunningham walked to his fancy private school in Manhattan, completely unaware that something was about to happen that would change his life forever. The last thing Claude expected when he arrived at the Worthington School was to meet the person who was going to turn him into a hero, but life has a funny way of taking major turns when you least expect them. In this case, the major, unexpected turn in Claude's life came in the form of a substitute teacher named Flora Rattlebee.

It was uncommon to have a substitute teacher at the Worthington School. The teachers, like the students, were expected to be in optimal health, work hard, and never miss school. But that morning, Claude spotted a tiny woman in the hallway and heard Mr. Frool, his myopic (meaning nearsighted rather than narrow-minded) history teacher, call out to her from across the hallway.

"Excuse me! Are you an exchange student? Can I help you?" Mr. Frool said in his condescending way.

The little woman laughed, and in a very high, childlike voice responded, "No, no. I'm Ms. Rattlebee! I'm substituting for Mr. Bryant. He was hit by a taxi this past weekend."

"Hit by a taxi! My goodness!" cried Mr. Frool, reddening a bit because he mistook the middle-aged Ms. Rattlebee for a student simply because she was so short. "Is he all right?"

"Well, I'm afraid he's not all right," Ms. Rattlebee replied in the way one might speak to a young child. "He was *hit by a taxi.* He's in the hospital, and I'm told he *will* be all right, but he'll be recovering all week."

"I see then," replied a flustered and irritated Mr. Frool. "You'll want to head over to the seventh-grade room." Mr. Frool then turned away and strode down the hall, leaving Ms. Rattlebee wondering where the room was. She looked a bit lost, so Claude, who'd heard the whole exchange, walked up to her and introduced himself.

"Hello, Ms. Rattlebee," he said, looking way down at the little woman, who, he noticed, was wearing a skirt made entirely out of sewn-together neckties and was carrying an enormous patchwork bag that was almost as big as she was. "I'm Claude Maxwell-Cunningham, and I'm in Mr. Bryant's class. I can show you where the room is. Can I carry your bag for you?"

"Why thank you, Claude," Ms. Rattlebee replied, handing him the bag and following him up a flight of stairs and down another hall to a door marked "7th Grade."

When they walked into the classroom, Ms. Rattlebee turned to Claude to thank him for being helpful, but Claude had stopped paying attention to her. He was preoccupied by his classmates' open-mouthed stares as they watched

Ms. Rattlebee enter the room. Ms. Rattlebee may have been accustomed to looking up at everyone, but these twelve-year-olds were not accustomed to looking down at grown-ups, especially not that far down. Nor had they ever seen a teacher dressed in such unusual clothes.

"Please be seated at your desks," she told the students, who were too flummoxed to do anything else but obey. "I'll take the bag now, Claude. Thank you," she said quietly, and the rest of the students' eyes followed Claude as he made his way to his chair.

"I'm Flora Rattlebee, and I will be filling in for Mr. Bryant this week. I'm afraid Mr. Bryant has been in an accident. He was hit by a taxicab this past weekend, and he is recovering in the hospital." And then Ms. Rattlebee whispered to herself in a voice that was still audible to everyone, "Poor man, smooshed by a taxi, terrible thing."

It was shocking enough to hear that their homeroom teacher had been hit by a taxi, but to hear the news from a teeny woman with the voice of a child, who wore a skirt made of ties, and who talked to herself, threw the students for quite a loop.

"Since Mr. Bryant did not expect to be hit by a taxi, I'm afraid he hasn't left me with his lesson plans, so you'll forgive me if today's class is a little different from what you're used to," Ms. Rattlebee began. "I'd like to start our class by introducing you to a friend of mine. Her name is Grinwhistle, and she has been traveling with me to visit schools for the past couple of weeks. She is doing research to try to understand some things about us. She likes talking to people your age because she says you tend to be very forthright and honest with her, which helps her gather the information she needs. So, are you willing to talk to her?"

The kids in Claude's class glanced around at each other, each one trying to decide how they should answer. The person who finally did respond to Ms. Rattlebee's question was Claude, our soon-to-be hero, and perhaps now's a good time to tell you why Claude would be so quick to reply to Ms. Rattlebee. Claude's mother, Helen Maxwell, was a United States senator, and his father, Farnsworth Cunningham, was an anchor on a national news station. Claude's famous parents weren't home much, and Claude's sister, Olivia, was seven years older than he and attending Princeton University, so Claude barely saw her, either. This meant that Claude was cared for by Marisa, the housekeeper, and Sophie, the cook, both of whom doted on Claude. His every need was attended to, and he was free to do just about anything, as long as it would reflect well upon the Maxwell-Cunninghams.

Claude was expected to earn good grades, and he did. He was expected to be a good sport (and good at sports), and he was. He was expected to be well-liked among his peers, and he was elected class president. He was expected to be polite at all times, and his parents bragged that his very first word was "please." He was a handsome, easy-to-get-along-with twelve-year-old. Thus, Claude was polite to Ms. Rattlebee and was the first to reply, "Sure, we'll talk to your friend."

Now it might sound like Claude was a great guy, and the kind of kid you would want to be friends with, but there's a bit more to tell you. Claude was popular because it suited him to be so. He watched how his mother said just what people wanted to hear so that she would get their votes, and he became a skillful politician himself. He wanted to get into Princeton one day, like his sister and his parents and grandparents, so he worked hard enough to get the grades he would need. He loved sports and realized that good sportsmanship went a long way toward success. He did what he did primarily to make his own life better, not because he really wanted to do the right thing or because he was particularly caring towards others. If you had met Claude before the changes that were about to take place, you probably would have liked him, but you may not have felt that he could become a good friend. You might have enjoyed his company, but you might not have gotten the feeling you could talk to him if something was wrong. In fact, although Claude was very popular, he really had no *close* friends at all.

"Great! I'll get Grinwhistle then!" responded an enthusiastic Ms. Rattlebee.

Ms. Rattlebee did not, however, leave the room to get her friend. Instead, she stood in front of the class, closed her eyes, began swaying back and forth, twitched a few times, and then suddenly opened her eyes and stared at the students, looking even stranger than before.

"Greetings, Earthlings," the voice coming out of Ms. Rattlebee's mouth said. "I am Grinwhistle, from a planet many light-years away. I travel in the form of energy, and I've entered Ms. Rattlebee's body so that I might speak to you and ask you questions. I'm here on a fact-finding mission. On my planet, all beings are treated with respect and compassion, and I want to know how others behave on different planets. Will you tell me how I'm supposed to behave in your world?"

By now the students thought that Ms. Rattlebee was insane. Will Wingfield, who was the tallest boy in the seventh grade and always acted as if middle school was beneath him (which it kind of was, given his height), rolled his eyes, and Austin McKenzie, who spent his afternoons playing tennis at his family's tennis club, snorted audibly. Penelope Brewster, who was popular primarily because most of the girls were afraid of her, said with a smirk on her face, "Sure we will, *Grinwhistle.*"

"Very good. On your planet, how are you supposed to treat other people?"

Penelope's voice dripped with sarcasm as she replied, "The way you would want to be treated." At this, the few girls in the class who were not followers of Penelope Brewster looked at her in amazement, since Penelope didn't generally treat people nicely.

"Does everyone agree with that?" asked Grinwhistle, and most of the class nodded.

"Wonderful!" shouted Grinwhistle. "That's how it is on my planet! So, I assume that you would never harm each other, right?"

"Well, sometimes. I mean if someone hurts you, then you can hurt them back. And some people are bullies," said Lucas Christiansen, a slight boy with wire-rimmed glasses who snuck a glance at Brent Sklar, who had a reputation as the class bully.

"Well, that's odd," responded Grinwhistle. "I thought you were supposed to treat each other the way you want to be treated. I can't imagine anyone would want to be bullied! Well, let me ask you this: I've noticed that people on your planet are all different shapes and sizes and colors. How do you treat those who are different from you, let's say who have a different skin color, or who are very big or very little?"

Most of the students looked down when Grinwhistle asked this, realizing how much they had been judging Ms. Rattlebee because of her size. Plus, there were only five kids out of twenty in the class who weren't white: Zahra Kanumba from Tanzania; Lee Chong, whose parents were from China; Meeta Bannerjee, whose family was originally from India; Isaak Washington-Nasr, who had a Black mom and an Iranian mom; and Medea Ramon, whose background nobody knew much about. There was an awkward moment as the kids tried to figure out how to talk about racism with Ms. Rattlebee's strange alien alter ego.

Medea, whom pretty much everyone considered the smartest kid in the class (and who was another soon-to-be hero), broke the silence. "We're supposed to treat everyone equally, but sometimes we don't. Some people are prejudiced against others because of things like skin color. For hundreds of years, the United States enslaved Black people, and even after the Civil War and the Emancipation Proclamation that officially ended slavery, our government created racist laws and policies. The problem with people is that we don't always *follow* the golden rule to treat others the way we'd want to be treated," she finished, her voice fading as she noticed her classmates looking at her like it was ridiculous to play along with Grinwhistle.

"Why on Earth would people care what color your skin is? How utterly arbitrary and bizarre!" cried Grinwhistle. "On our planet, no one cares what color or pattern you are.

"Well, let me ask about something else. How are you supposed to treat other species on your planet—for instance, birds? I noticed some lovely sparrows flying outside when I arrived this morning."

"Oh, we're supposed to treat them nicely!" cried Samantha Curry, who had dimples and rosy cheeks. "At my grandmother's house in Connecticut, we put out birdseed, and so many birds come to the feeders."

"That's good to hear! It's similar on my planet. We always share our food with others. So, you treat all birds this way then?"

"Well, not *all* birds," piped up Tony Melina, who was known for stirring things up.

"What do you mean?" asked Samantha.

"We eat some of them; I mean, you eat chicken, Samantha. I've seen you."

"Are they really birds, though?" Samantha asked, turning rosier than usual. "I mean, they're food."

"You eat them?" asked a perplexed Grinwhistle. "I thought you said you were supposed to treat them nicely. That's what you said about other people, too. Do you also eat each other?"

"Of course not!" exclaimed Samantha.

"So why do you eat chickens, but not sparrows?"

"Because they taste good," Tony answered.

"Sparrows don't taste good?"

"I don't know. I've never tried them," he responded, getting exasperated.

"Why not?" Grinwhistle inquired.

"Because we don't eat sparrows!" he practically yelled.

Grinwhistle sighed. "This is confusing. Tell me about dogs. I noticed some people walking dogs on the street. Do you eat them as well?"

"No!" shouted several kids, but then Tony, looking pointedly at Lee Chong, quipped, "In some countries, people eat dogs."

"How is that any different from eating pigs? They're as smart as dogs," Lee retorted.

"But pigs are for food. Dogs aren't!" cried Samantha, looking a bit shaken.

"Pigs aren't food to some Jews and Muslims," interjected Peter Levy, who was Jewish, and whose grandparents kept kosher.

Then Medea spoke up again.

"Basically, most people eat the animals that they were raised to eat. It has nothing to do with how smart the animals are, or even how cute they are. There's no important difference between sparrows and chickens or between pigs and dogs. It's not about them; it's about how we feel about them."

The class was silent for a moment, and then Grinwhistle turned to Medea. "That sounds quite arbitrary, too. I'd hate to be born a pig or chicken in your world."

Then with a somewhat pained expression on her face, Grinwhistle added, "I'm afraid I must go now. But thank you for answering my questions. I certainly have a lot to think about."

Her voice faded as she waved goodbye to the class, closed her eyes, and twitched and swayed in Ms. Rattlebee's tiny body.

A moment later, Ms. Rattlebee's eyes opened.

She appeared a bit woozy after the experience of having her body "occupied" by an alien. With her high voice, she asked the class, "So, what did you think of my friend Grinwhistle?"

What was there to say? Most of the students thought that Rattlebee's Grinwhistle act was bizarre.

Will Wingfield scoffed. "I thought she was weird and dumb."

Some of the other kids laughed and gave Will the thumbs up for saying what they were too scared, or perhaps too polite, to say.

"Ah well. Grinwhistle sometimes asks questions that people don't really want to think about," Ms. Rattlebee replied, and Will's face looked a bit less cocky at the implied slight.

Then, she asked the class to think about Medea's comment and write down why they think we call some animals pets and others food. Claude was thankful for the opportunity to collect his thoughts.

You may remember that Claude had no close friends. That isn't quite true. Claude had no close *human* friends. He did, however, have a best friend and that was Rooper, his beautiful, loyal, and absolutely adoring dog. The thought of someone eating Rooper made Claude sick to his stomach and got him thinking about things he'd never thought about before. Why *was* it okay to eat some animals and not others? What really *was* the difference? He didn't know any pigs personally, but what if he did? What if he had a friend like Rooper who happened to be a pig?

At lunch that day, the kids in Claude's class were snidely laughing about Ms. Rattlebee and the class she'd taught. Samantha was going off about birds, arguing that chickens didn't really count because they weren't wild. Penelope talked about how astonishing it was that anyone with such preposterous ideas would be allowed to teach their class and said it was an insult to their intelligence. No one seemed to be thinking about the questions Ms. Rattlebee had raised. Claude listened to his classmates, looked at his ham and cheese sandwich, lost his appetite, and put his food down.

Chapter 2

Medea's life was very different from the other students at Worthington. She couldn't buy what she wanted or go on vacations during school holidays. And while most of the kids at Worthington spent their weekends at their country clubs or second homes in the Hamptons and their summers at sleepaway camps in Maine, Medea spent her weekends and summers with her friends in her East Harlem neighborhood. Although Medea had been attending the Worthington School for two years, she'd never made any friends there, and no one really knew anything about her.

Medea lived with her father, who worked as a doorman at a swanky Fifth Avenue apartment building. Her mom had died from cancer when she was a toddler, and shortly thereafter she and her dad moved from their home in Puerto Rico to New York City. For as long as she could remember, it had just been her and her dad. Marvin Ramon was a great dad who tried his best to be both mother and father to Medea. When she was little, he brought her to the library on Saturday afternoons and let her pick out piles of books to bring home. He'd read to her every night after dinner, then tuck her into bed. One evening, when Medea was five, he went back into her room about a half hour after they'd said good night, just because he wanted to look at her sweet face as she slept. He was shocked to discover that she was reading under the covers with a flashlight. And when I say reading, I don't mean that she was looking at the drawings in a picture book. No, Medea was actually reading *The Boxcar Children*, which hardly had any pictures in it at all. That's when Marvin realized that Medea was really smart.

Medea attended a public school in their neighborhood, which, shockingly, was referred to as "the rubble pit" or "pit" for short, because it was literally falling apart, and students had to share their books and sometimes even their desks. Marvin knew that Medea was bored and frustrated there, but he couldn't find an apartment near his work with a better public school. The apartments on the Upper East Side, where he was a doorman, were far more expensive than he could afford on his salary, and he didn't want to move any farther away because he wanted to be close enough to Medea's school so that he could meet her shortly after the school day was over. The public school in their neighborhood was only a thirty-minute walk or ten-minute bus ride from his job.

When Medea was in fourth grade, she had a teacher who was truly wonderful—the kind of teacher who loves every child and does everything she can to help each one learn in the way that they learn best. But although she was a terrific teacher, she couldn't do enough for Medea. Medea was so far ahead of her classmates, and there was no way that she could give Medea the attention she needed, not with more than thirty other children in her class. She'd even had Medea tutor her classmates, hoping to challenge her and give her something meaningful to do, but that didn't solve the problem of Medea not getting the education she deserved. So Medea's teacher called Marvin to set up a meeting and told him tearfully (because she believed deeply in public education and was dismayed that their school had so few resources, such big classes, and so many challenges that it was impossible to meet Medea's needs) that Medea really needed to go to a different school.

When Marvin told Medea's teacher his dilemma, she said that Medea was *so* smart she felt certain she would receive a full scholarship at one of the private schools on Manhattan's Upper East Side near his work. She even offered to help Marvin apply. Marvin didn't want to abandon their public school or have Medea leave her neighborhood and her friends every day, but he did want Medea to get the best possible education. It wasn't easy to make the decision he did, but he decided to apply to the Worthington School.

That's how Medea came to attend one of the most exclusive schools in the country. Although she missed her friends, Medea loved Worthington. The classes were small. There was state-of-the-art equipment, including 3-D printers and smart boards. There were computers with all the software she could ever want and endless opportunities to learn. Medea knew that she had to be good, get straight As, and stay out of any sort of trouble if she was going to keep her scholarship. She understood that if she lost it, her father would never be able to afford Worthington, and although she was often lonely, going to Worthington meant everything to her.

You might imagine that Medea had nothing to worry about. After all, she was so smart, and she loved learning, so all the teachers were bound to like her. You would be right, except for one teacher—Mr. Frool. Remember when I told you that Mr. Frool was myopic, meaning nearsighted rather than narrow-minded? He was also myopic meaning narrow-minded rather than nearsighted. He had this snobbish idea that only kids whose parents were wealthy should go to Worthington. In his mind, the child of a doorman shouldn't attend such an elite school for privileged children. Mr. Frool spent an inordinate amount of time watching Medea, just waiting for her to do something wrong, bad, or sneaky so that the school would take away her scholarship and she'd be forced to leave. Medea knew that Mr. Frool didn't like her, although she didn't understand why, and so she tried extra hard not to make any waves. She was good, good, good.

For years, Marvin had worked from 7:30 a.m. to 3:30 p.m. at 1055 Fifth Avenue. Once Medea started going to Worthington, he dropped her off at school at 7:20, and she sat quietly with the receptionist and worked on her homework until school began. She waited again at the end of the day for Marvin to meet her after he was done with work. When she entered seventh grade, however, Marvin was unexpectedly put on the evening shift. The superintendent of the building had a cousin who wanted to work during the days, and Marvin got bumped to nights. In the afternoons he was still able to be with Medea (who by seventh grade walked home from school by herself), and to fix their dinner and hang out before bed, but now he had to leave her alone at nights. Neither he nor Medea liked this new arrangement, but they adjusted to it.

The day after Ms. Rattlebee arrived at their school, Medea didn't want to sit alone at lunch as she usually did. Ms. Rattlebee, who was still substituting for Mr. Bryant, had just told them about something that was so awful and so unbelievable that Medea thought she would burst if she didn't talk to somebody. Ms. Rattlebee had described children her age who were working as slaves. Slaves! Hadn't Medea—just the day before—talked about how slavery had ended? How was it possible that slavery still existed in the 21st century?!

Ms. Rattlebee had started the class by handing a sheet of paper to each student and telling them to read it quietly. The room was silent, except for occasional gasps. Medea read about Kumar, a boy in India who worked all day, every day, tying knots in rugs. His whole body became deformed because he was bent over twelve hours a day, week after week, year after year. He never got to go to school, was always hungry, and hadn't seen his parents in four years!

Medea assumed that her classmates were all reading about Kumar, too, but after a few minutes, Ms. Rattlebee had the class divide up into groups and asked each student to tell the others in their group about the child they'd read about. That's when Medea realized that each one of them had read a different story, about a different child. There were 20 different stories, 20 separate kids from all over the world living as slaves. When a student in Medea's group spoke about Martina, a girl from Bolivia who was a servant for a wealthy family in Los Angeles, Medea was dumbfounded. She couldn't understand how anyone could get away with that. She had no idea that children were forced to work as servants in the United States. She thought Ms. Rattlebee must be exaggerating the stories. Then the bell rang before Medea had a chance to ask Ms. Rattlebee all the questions that were whirring inside her mind.

After class, Medea got on her computer to find out if what Ms. Rattlebee had told them was true or exaggerated. After 25 minutes of reading information from several reputable news sources, Medea learned that Ms. Rattlebee had told them the truth. Not surprisingly, she was very upset. That's why she really wanted to find someone to talk to at lunch. But when she went down to the cafeteria and approached one of the tables where the girls in her class were eating, she overheard Penelope saying, "Isn't Rattlebee supposed to be following a Worthington *curriculum*? I don't actually think what she's teaching is *appropriate*. My mother was *apoplectic* when I told her about that Grinwhistle thing she did yesterday. She said she'd be calling the principal if Rattlebee kept this up. I can't wait to tell her what she did today. That was *appalling*." (Penelope liked to use big words, especially those that started with the letter *a*.)

Medea sighed and realized that she had no one to talk to after all, so she sat by herself as usual. But because she wanted to get as far away from Penelope as possible, she wound up sitting next to the popular boys' table. Too preoccupied with Ms. Rattlebee's class to do her homework while she ate, she didn't attempt to tune out the cacophony of the lunchroom as she typically did. So, when she heard raised voices coming from the table next to her, she listened to every word.

Over at the boys' table, Claude was steaming inside. He'd never been so angry in his life, and he wasn't sure what to make of these unfamiliar feelings. Claude simply wasn't used to thinking much about other people (except to consider how they might be of help to him). Now, because of some strange substitute teacher and her even stranger classes, he was beset with emotions about suffering children who lived halfway around the world. It was hard enough thinking about people eating dogs the day before; now he was thinking about people enslaving children! It was just too much for the normally carefree Claude to fit into his otherwise pleasant view of the world, and he quite suddenly discovered that it was no longer possible to think only of himself in the face of other children's misery.

Claude was amazed that the other boys at the table, which included Will Wingfield, Austin McKenzie, and Tony Melina, didn't seem similarly upset. Not only that, but they were making fun of Ms. Rattlebee. Will crouched down in his chair pretending to be Rattlebee and mimicked her voice, saying, "I just escaped from a mental hospital, so excuse me for telling you about my hallucinations!"

Austin and Tony were laughing, and Will added, "Yes, and don't mind my homemade clothes. I can't afford real clothes."

Finally, Claude couldn't stand it anymore, and all his thoughts and feelings just burst out. Speaking very quickly and unusually loudly, he exclaimed, "Who cares about her clothes?! What about what she's teaching us? This slavery thing must be illegal. I'm going to talk to my mom so that she can propose a law to stop it. And I'm going to ask my dad to do a report about it on the news, too."

The boys just stared at Claude. Claude rarely mentioned his famous parents or sounded mad.

Austin, still tan from sailing all summer, broke the silence that had descended upon their table by telling Claude to lighten up.

Will piped in, "Yeah, who knows if Rattlebee is even telling the truth about all that. I mean, she's kind of nuts, Claude. Have you ever seen a slave in New York? She's probably making it up."

"Hey, at least we haven't had any homework with Rattlebee," Austin added.

"I don't care about whether she gave us homework! Don't you think we ought to do something about this?"

"Claude, chill. You're taking this stuff way too seriously," said Austin, who was trying to soothe Claude and calm things down.

Claude could see that his friends were looking at him very strangely, like he'd lost his mind. That was the last thing Claude wanted, but he was all conflicted inside. He didn't know what to make of the anger he felt at his classmates, or the sadness he felt about what Ms. Rattlebee had taught him. He was Claude Maxwell-Cunningham, the popular, easygoing class president. Trying to save face and collect himself, he turned to the other boys, flashed his great smile, and said, "Yeah, I guess so. Hey, speaking of homework, I'd better get my math done; I didn't do it last night. See you guys later."

Chapter 3

Medea was very careful and deliberate and rarely acted impulsively at school, but when she saw Claude get up and leave his friends, she gathered her mostly uneaten lunch and her computer and quickly followed him out of the lunchroom. He was moving so fast that she had to run to catch up with him. He headed down a hallway that led to the garden, a small courtyard that was seldom used by the students. By the time she opened the heavy steel door, she was breathless.

Claude wheeled around at the sound of the door, startled that anyone might be coming into the garden. He'd been coming here for years when he wanted to be alone, and he'd never encountered anyone else.

"Hi," Medea said, panting.

"Hi," replied Claude, now even more surprised by the situation. "Um, are you okay?"

"Oh. Yes. Absolutely. I mean, not exactly. I mean, I heard what you said at lunch, and I completely agree with you. I can't stop thinking about what Ms. Rattlebee told us, and I'm so glad you said something."

Claude was completely taken aback. He'd never had a conversation with Medea, and no one he knew had ever talked to Medea outside of class. Claude had always thought she was arrogant, and now here she was stumbling over her words, out of breath, and, was he right about this—was she actually blushing?

"Thanks. I felt a little stupid after my outburst." Claude paused, not sure exactly what to say but happy to have someone to talk to.

"Well, I don't think it was stupid at all. I'm so relieved that someone else cares!"

This comment was a little hard for Claude to take in. He did care about the enslaved children, and he hadn't been able to eat meat since the day before, but Claude wasn't used to being described as "someone who cares." He didn't know quite what to say but figured if he mentioned that he hadn't eaten meat, that would at least show that maybe she was right about him caring.

"You know, I haven't been able to eat meat since yesterday. I had a peanut butter and jelly sandwich today for lunch."

"Really? I've been a vegetarian since I read *Charlotte's Web* when I was six, so I haven't been thinking about yesterday's class much, but what she told us today—that was awful." Medea was speaking quickly, and not sure what else she should say, she thought she'd try asking Claude a question to get him to talk more. "So, who was your story about this morning?"

Glad to be able to talk about something specific, Claude told her about Neem, the Pakistani child he'd learned about who made bricks every day in the blazing hot sun. "Every day, even on weekends, even on holidays. Just making brick after brick after brick, forever." Claude was still focused on what Medea had said about reading *Charlotte's Web*, and he wanted to find out more about that, and about her, so he added: "You've been a vegetarian since you were six? I didn't know that."

"Well, how would you? It's not like I hang out with anyone here. None of you know anything about me," Medea responded, her tone shifting into what Claude had always perceived as snobby.

"Right. Why is that, anyway? You think you're better than the rest of us because you're so smart?" retorted Claude, suddenly far less friendly than normal.

"*Better* than you? You think that's what I think? Claude, I live in East Harlem, and my dad works at 1055 Fifth Avenue, where he opens the door every day for kids who probably go to this school," Medea said with a tight, controlled voice and smoldering eyes that bore into Claude. And without further comment, she turned around and walked out of the garden.

When Medea was back in the building, she could feel her heart pounding. She felt such a mixture of emotions—anger, hurt, embarrassment, confusion. Here was this rich, popular kid with famous parents implying that she was a snob for keeping to herself, when really she was just scared of being rejected by the other kids! She didn't feel comfortable inviting Worthington students over to her small apartment, and she kept quiet about her background. What on Earth had she been thinking when she told Claude about her dad's job! She wanted to kick herself for being so stupid. Was he going to tell the other kids, and would they make fun of her? She couldn't stand that! Her father was the best man in the world, as far as she was concerned. But somehow, furious as she was at Claude, and angry as she was at herself for talking about her dad's job, she also believed that Claude might be trustworthy. He actually cared about those children they'd learned about that day, and he hadn't eaten meat since yesterday's class. That meant something.

CHAPTER 4

Claude's jaw dropped open, and he shook his head. Was this real? Had he really been followed by a breathless Medea Ramon, the brainy class snob, insulted her, and heard her say that her father worked at 1055 Fifth Avenue? Claude lived at 1055 Fifth Avenue, and he realized he knew Medea's father, Marvin Ramon. Marvin was the kind doorman who helped him when his backpack was heavy, flagged a taxi for him when he needed one, and was now working the night shift, stifling a yawn in the mornings before he got off work. He could barely believe what had just happened, and he was filled with a mixture of shame and annoyance. Medea *did* act like she was better than the rest of them, but thinking about Marvin made him feel uncomfortable, and he wasn't entirely sure why.

Claude couldn't concentrate during the rest of his classes that day, or even during soccer practice after school. He walked home from school feeling unsettled and confused by his emotions. He wished he had someone to talk to about everything that had happened in the last two days, but his mother was in Washington, and his father wouldn't get home until nine that night.

When Claude got home, Rooper ran to the door and wagged his whole body in greeting. He licked Claude's face, did a little dance with his feet, and made a howling sound like "woah woah woah woah," which Claude translated as, "I'm so glad you're home! I missed you so much, and now I'm the happiest dog in the world!" Rooper threw himself over onto his back and wiggled his body to tell Claude to rub his tummy. Usually this worked, although sometimes, when Claude was in a rush or preoccupied, he'd just step over Rooper. That's when Rooper would roll himself back around, get up, run in front of Claude and try again. Some days, Claude would still ignore him and disappear into the kitchen to get something to eat, but today was not one of those days. Claude got down on the floor with Rooper and pet his belly for a long time. It was Claude's responsibility to walk Rooper in the afternoons, and usually he'd wait until after he'd had a snack, and then walk him into the park, let him relieve himself, and turn right around, but today he decided he would take Rooper on a walk right away.

"Want to go out, Rooper?" Claude asked him, and Rooper jumped and scampered around the foyer, grabbed his leash in his mouth, and dashed out the door the moment Claude opened it. Claude and Rooper entered Central Park, and Rooper quickly peed and started to turn back, but Claude said, "Let's keep walking, Rooper," and Rooper leapt up with excitement. He led Claude on a long outing all the way to the rowing pond, around the trails, and back to the Alice in Wonderland statue, where he lay down under the giant mushroom to rest. Claude found himself remembering the fun he'd had in the park as a child. He thought about the years he used to go rowing with Marisa out on the pond, dragging his toes in the water, and about the times he would climb on top of Alice's head. He made a promise to himself to take Rooper on a good walk every day and stop ignoring him so much.

When they got back home, Claude went into the kitchen to get his snack.

"Hi Sophie, what's for dinner tonight?"

"Oh, I made your favorite, Claudie—lamb chops, mashed potatoes, and green beans."

"Oh." Claude's heart sank. "Thanks, Sophie. Hey Sophie, I think I'd like to try being vegetarian, okay? Would you mind? Can we have spaghetti tomorrow?"

"Vegetarian? I don't know, Claudie. You have to ask your parents."

"I'll talk to them, Sophie. But tomorrow, spaghetti and tomato sauce, okay?"

Claude went to his room with Rooper, patted his bed for Rooper to jump up, and sat with him for a long time trying to decide what to do. He wanted to talk to Medea, but thinking about it made him nervous. She might not want to talk to him, and he didn't know what he should say. But he thought and thought and planned every word, and somehow all that thinking about it made him feel he had to get it over with. He didn't know her cell phone number, so he found her online and messaged her.

Hi, Medea. I'm really sorry I thought you were a snob. You're just so smart I figured you thought we were all too stupid for you. Oh, and I live at 1055 Fifth Avenue. I know your dad, Marvin. I'm one of the kids he opens the door for. I really like your dad. He's the nicest doorman who works here. I mean really nice. He must be a great dad. Do you think maybe we could get together after soccer practice tomorrow to talk about Ms. Rattlebee and everything she's taught us? My number is 917-555-0199. Please text me.

And then he waited. He tried to do his homework, but he couldn't concentrate. Finally, just before dinner, he got a text.

Okay.

Claude had no idea what Medea was thinking or feeling, but he figured she must have forgiven him, or she wouldn't have said "okay." He didn't realize just how relieved he was until his mom called from Washington, commented that he sounded happy, and asked him about school.

Even though two hours ago he would've been so glad to talk to his mom and tell her about Ms. Rattlebee and ask her about what could be done about slavery, he realized that he didn't want to go into any of it at that moment. He was going to talk to Medea tomorrow, and for now he thought he'd just keep the events of the past couple of days to himself.

"School's good. Rooper and I went on a long walk this afternoon. We walked to Alice."

"Oh, Alice. I always loved her. Remember how you used to sit on the Mad Hatter's hat?"

"Yup. Hey Mom, I wanted to ask you something. I'd like to become a vegetarian. Sophie says it's up to you and dad. Can you ask her to cook vegetarian food for me from now on?"

Claude knew that when his mother was in Washington, she was more likely to say yes to Claude's requests because she felt guilty about being away. Asking his mother was definitely a better choice than waiting until his dad came home after a long day and night's work.

"Why do you want to be a vegetarian, Claude?"

"I just don't want to eat animals anymore. I wouldn't eat Rooper, so I thought, 'Why should I eat other animals?'"

"Hmm. I guess that's okay, but I want to make sure that Sophie prepares balanced meals for you." Thinking out loud, Claude's mother added, "Senator Stevens is vegetarian, and he seems quite healthy. I'll ask him about his diet. But in the meantime, I'll let Sophie know that it's fine for you to be vegetarian. Be good, Claude. I'll talk to you tomorrow."

"Okay. Bye, Mom."

Claude talked to his mom almost every evening, and usually the conversations were short and easy. She didn't bug him about his homework or violin practice, but she left that for Marisa to do.

Claude sighed and realized he might as well get his homework and practicing done without waiting for Marisa to nag him, which he knew she hated to do. Not only did Marisa love Claude (almost as much as his parents), but she also paid very close attention to him (even more than his parents).

CHAPTER 5

The next day, Claude passed Medea in the hallway and tried to catch her eye, but she ignored him, not even glancing his way. He thought that was weird but was quickly distracted as he walked into the seventh-grade room and saw Ms. Rattlebee standing on Mr. Bryant's desk, wearing what looked like a burlap sack with a rope for a belt and holding a big garbage bag in her hand.

When everyone was sitting at their desks, Ms. Rattlebee, who had not yet said a word, opened the garbage bag, turned it upside down, and let the contents spill all over the floor. There were Styrofoam pieces, plastic milk containers, disposable water bottles, a piece of rope, and various plastic junk strewn about their classroom floor, and a smiling Ms. Rattlebee perched atop the desk.

"What do you think all that is?" she asked the class, pointing to the mess on the floor with an eagerness in her voice that made it sound even higher than usual.

"Uh, *garbage*," answered Penelope with obvious sarcasm.

"Absolutely right, Penelope!" squeaked Ms. Rattlebee. "And do you know where this garbage came from?"

"A garbage *bag*?" she replied, smirking.

"You're a smart one, Penelope Brewster. But this garbage *didn't* come from a garbage bag. I just put it in a garbage bag so that I could carry it. This garbage was found inside the stomach of a twenty-eight-foot baleen whale. Well, not this exact garbage, but garbage just like it. The whale was found dead on a beach in North Carolina. She had been feeding in the ocean, opening her huge mouth to catch the tiny krill that make up most of her diet, and these bits of garbage entered her mouth and were trapped when she strained the water out of her baleen. She swallowed all this trash, and it killed her." Then, speaking to herself, she murmured, "poor whale," but as usual, everyone heard this, too.

"How do you know that's what killed her?" Penelope asked, skeptical about Ms. Rattlebee's story.

"Wildlife veterinarians did a necropsy and determined that she starved to death because her stomach was full of garbage instead of food, that's how we know. Now, here's what I want you to do," Ms. Rattlebee continued. "Everyone, come up and pick up a piece of garbage and bring it to your desk."

No one moved.

"Come on, it won't bite you!"

Catching Penelope's disgusted look, Ms. Rattlebee smiled at her and added, "Don't worry, Penelope, it's all nice, clean, *disinfected* garbage."

Penelope took her purse out of her desk and rummaged around in it until she found a pair of tweezers, which she used to pick up a plastic six-pack ring from the pile of garbage on the floor. When all the students had a piece of trash on their desk, Ms. Rattlebee asked the class to do three things: first, to get on their computers and do some quick research to get a sense of the effects of their piece of garbage on the environment; next, to consider whether their item was a "want" or a "need." Her final request was to think about what else could have been done with it so that it didn't wind up in a whale's stomach. Then she issued a strange command: "Think like a solutionary!"

Claude was thoroughly enjoying the class and surreptitiously glanced over at Medea and noticed that her eyes were bright and her attention riveted on Ms. Rattlebee. Most of the other kids, however, were handling their piece of trash like it was nuclear waste.

After about thirty minutes, Ms. Rattlebee asked the students to report on their items. It was fascinating to Claude how many effects these simple objects could have. Whenever students thought they'd come up with everything, Ms. Rattlebee would rattle off a few more ways in which the item, as well as all the processes involved in producing it, might be affecting the environment. And she always had another few ideas about what else one could do with it. When Tony Melina, who had the piece of rope, said you could reuse it instead of throwing it away, Ms. Rattlebee grabbed the rope around her waist and exclaimed, "Indeed, they make good belts!"

At this, Penelope actually guffawed.

Ms. Rattlebee turned to her. "I may not care very much about fashion, Penelope, but I do care very much about our beautiful Earth. That's why I reuse things, and why I make many of my clothes."

Emboldened by her growing disdain for Ms. Rattlebee (and by her mother's promise that if Ms. Rattlebee didn't start following the Worthington curriculum, she'd have a word with the head of the school), Penelope sneered, "Like that skirt made out of ties?"

A wave of sadness passed over Ms. Rattlebee's face, and she spoke in a faraway voice. "Those were my husband's ties. I made that skirt after he died last year. It's my very favorite thing to wear."

Penelope lowered her head, and for a moment she actually looked ashamed.

"Back to our task at hand, yes?" Ms. Rattlebee said, recovering her composure. "Let's hear some more about your pieces of trash, shall we?"

The students continued to report on their items. Many of them said that their piece of garbage was a "need," although Claude thought that everything in the trash bag was really a "want." When it came right down to it, they didn't really need all this stuff, they just liked it because it made life more convenient. Claude's head was spinning again. He'd never thought much about the things he bought or used, or what effects they might have. He admired Ms. Rattlebee for making a skirt out of her late husband's ties. He thought that was pretty creative, and even though the skirt was definitely odd, he found it strangely beautiful. He started thinking about all the things he could reuse, too. Despite how unsettled he felt, he liked all this thinking.

Medea continued to ignore Claude all day, and when school and soccer practice were over, Claude had to wait until every single kid had left the building before she appeared.

"Okay, let's go." Medea was cheery and acted as if everything were normal and she hadn't been ignoring him all day.

"I hope it's okay with you, but I need to pick up my dog to walk him. We can take him to the park," said Claude.

"Okay," said Medea, who felt a little funny about going to her dad's place of employment with a boy from the building, even though her dad wouldn't be working there until that night.

After they picked up Rooper, Medea brought up the fact that she'd ignored Claude all day. "I don't want you to think I'm being rude or anything. I just think it's better if no one at school thinks we're friends." She stumbled a bit on the word *friends*, reddening as she said it.

"Uh ... Why not?"

"People might not understand why we'd be spending time together. And I don't want anyone asking me too many questions about myself. It's not always easy for me at Worthington, you know. It's better if people just think I'm some sort of loner. It's simpler for me that way. Okay?"

Claude felt awkward again, not knowing what to say. He didn't really understand what Medea meant, but he also realized that he had no idea what it was like for Medea at Worthington. "Okay. But I think you may be judging the rest of us a little harshly. I don't care about where you live and stuff like that."

"That may be, Claude, but what about Penelope Brewster and her crowd of girls? What about Austin McKenzie and Will Wingfield? What do you think your friends would say if they knew you were hanging out with me? Anyway, let's talk about something else, okay? What did you think of today's class?"

Of course, Medea was talking about Ms. Rattlebee's class, the only class worth talking about.

"I liked it. It was fun thinking about what else I could do with the milk container. After class, I came up with this idea to cut the bottom off it, turn it upside down, and use it like a short lacrosse basket. You know, get a ball and make a bunch of them and catch and throw the ball that way. Wouldn't that be cool? We could reuse a lot of plastic containers."

"Yeah." Medea sounded less than enthusiastic. "But the thing is, I feel like we should be doing something more than that, something like that word Ms. Rattlebee used—*solutionary*. Don't get me wrong, Claude," she added, sensitive about sounding arrogant. "Your idea is great, but that whale *died*. And right now, while we're talking, there are millions of kids in the world working in horrible conditions, and thousands of animals getting killed this very instant. I don't just want to talk about this stuff; I want to do something that makes a difference!"

Claude looked at Medea and smiled as he realized that another one of his judgments was wrong. He'd thought that Medea was not only snobby, but also reserved and studious and detached. He'd had no idea how passionate she could be.

"What do you want to do?"

"I don't know yet, but whatever it is, I can't get into trouble. I go to Worthington on a scholarship, and I can't do anything that might risk it."

"Well, I'm with you on that. I may not be getting a scholarship, but I can't get in trouble, either. My parents are too famous, and my mom is up for reelection next year. She had a friend in the Senate whose teenage son got caught driving when he was drunk. She never won another election. My mother told me the story, and it was pretty clear that I better not do anything that would reflect poorly on her or my dad."

"Wow, that's a lot of pressure!" Medea said, surprised that a rich kid like Claude had to worry about anything.

"It's okay. I've never wanted to do anything that would get me in trouble anyway," Claude said, and laughed. Obeying rules and being courteous had been so ingrained in Claude that it had really never crossed his mind to rebel in any way.

"Hey Medea, I've decided to officially become a vegetarian."

"That's great, Claude," Medea responded, then paused for a second, realizing that she didn't want his friends to tease him or think he was weird. "Be careful whom you tell, though. The guys at Worthington may think that's a little strange. I wouldn't go around talking about it."

Claude was not used to keeping secrets. He'd never really had secrets to keep. Now he had three: his feelings about Ms. Rattlebee, his new friendship with Medea, and his vegetarianism.

"Well, now that we know that neither of us can get in trouble, what can we do?" Claude asked Medea.

"Not sure. I'll think about it. But I should go home now."

"All right. See you tomorrow, Medea," and with that they headed in opposite directions to walk to their respective homes.

Chapter 6

When Claude got to school the next morning, Ms. Rattlebee was standing outside the building's large oak doors with a big smile on her face. She said good morning and asked Claude to put his backpack inside the building, use the restroom if he needed to, and come right back out. As the rest of his classmates arrived, she asked them to do the same, until they were all gathered in front of the school.

"Follow me," she said as she walked with a skip in her step toward Central Park. "We're going on an outing!"

Normally, field trips were scheduled events, so this "outing" was unexpected. None of them had received permission slips for their parents to sign, and Penelope grimaced, as if trying to show that she was annoyed Ms. Rattlebee was breaking a school rule, but really, being outside on a beautiful morning with a mystery ahead of them wasn't all bad. Most of the kids seemed open to what might unfold, as if they were slowly getting used to, and perhaps even appreciating, Ms. Rattlebee and her strange lessons.

Ms. Rattlebee led them through the Engineer's Gate into Central Park and to a cherry tree next to the park's reservoir. The gnarly trunk looked ancient, and the swooping branches created a canopy under which she had them gather. She asked them to have a seat on the ground in a circle. Several kids glanced at one another, with a few, like Penelope, rolling their eyes, but they did what they were asked.

"You've learned some difficult things this week about the harm we cause other people and animals, so this morning I wanted to give you a gift. My hope is that long after I'm gone, today will serve as a reservoir into which you can dip for joy and awe. And truth be told, I also hope that this gift may compel you to protect our planet and all who reside here."

There was nothing about these particular words that was incomprehensible, but no one really had a clue what she was talking about. The concepts were too big, and the setting, while pretty, was not exactly awe-inspiring. This was still Manhattan, after all. What did it mean to have a "reservoir" to dip into for joy and awe? They couldn't even swim in the *actual* reservoir that had a huge fence around it. What could a metaphorical reservoir even be?

"Medea, would you mind being my partner for a demonstration?" Ms. Rattlebee asked.

It should come as no surprise that Medea didn't mind at all.

Ms. Rattlebee then asked Medea to close her eyes as she took her hand and supported her arm. She explained that she would be demonstrating the Wonder Walk, which was meant to awaken their senses. "After the demonstration," she said, "I will pair you up to do the activity yourselves."

She told them that they would take turns being the leader, and that the leader would introduce their partner to the natural world using their senses of seeing, hearing, touching, and smelling. Showing what she meant with Medea, she explained that tapping next to their partner's eye meant open your eyes to look; tapping their earlobe meant listen; placing their hands on something or placing something in their hands meant feel whatever they were touching; and tapping the tip of their nose meant take a deep sniff. "When necessary," she instructed, and then demonstrated with Medea, "you can gently angle your partner's head to look toward something or tap behind their knee to indicate that they should crouch down."

Ms. Rattlebee explained that they'd do the activity for ten minutes and then change roles, and that they should stay in sight and earshot so they would hear her whistle when it was time to switch. Then she added, "Once you are in pairs and have decided who will lead first, the entire activity must be done in complete silence."

"Any questions?" she asked, and perhaps because they were so unnerved and surprised by the strange activity, no one asked a thing.

Ms. Rattlebee then paired them up in ways that nobody expected. Members of cliques were broken up. She paired Brent Sklar with Lucas Christiansen and Lee Chong with Peter Levy. Claude and Medea both secretly hoped she would put them together, which she did. They tried not to smile too widely as they approached each other and held hands.

Medea offered to be the leader first, so Claude closed his eyes. He felt a combination of excitement and nervousness. Medea began to lead him slowly and carefully, and he found himself enjoying the trust he was placing in his new friend. He liked walking with his eyes closed and paying attention to the movement of his body in space.

Then Medea stopped and placed both of his hands on the tree they'd been sitting under. The bark felt bumpy, uneven, and rough. He moved his hands along its trunk, realizing that while he had passed this and the other cherry trees along the reservoir countless times before, he'd never really noticed them, and he felt strangely connected to the craggy old tree. He even had an impulse to wrap his arms around it, but he worried that would be too weird.

Next, Medea gently lifted his chin so that his head was facing up, and she tapped next to his eye. He opened his eyes and marveled at the sight above him. Some of the leaves were shimmying in the breeze, and he caught glimpses of the blue sky between them. He felt enveloped by the canopy, protected, surrounded by beauty. "How have I never really looked at something I've seen a million times?" he thought to himself. "This is the gift Ms. Rattlebee wanted us to have."

Medea took his hand to lead him somewhere else, and he closed his eyes. After a minute, she tapped next to his eyes again, and when he opened them, he saw a squirrel staring right at him, twitching his tail. What a big, fluffy tail he had! Then, the squirrel bounded off gracefully, and Claude closed his eyes again as Medea continued to lead him.

She positioned him to smell a flower, and the scent was intense and heady. Had he ever smelled a flower so deeply? Then she touched his earlobe, and he heard a blue jay screech and another bird make a melodious bell-like sound. She angled his head and tapped next to his eye. When he opened his eyes, there was the blue jay, but then the jay made the bell-like call. What? How had he not known that blue jays don't just screech but also sing?

Everything was amazing. Claude felt like he was experiencing the natural world for the very first time, as if all his senses had suddenly awakened after a long slumber. He felt as happy as he'd ever been. "This is what Ms. Rattlebee meant by joy," he thought.

Then Ms. Rattlebee whistled, and it was his turn to lead Medea. He was excited to find amazing things for her to experience, too. When he spotted a spider weaving a web—something he would probably never have noticed before that day—he positioned her just right to see the sun illuminate the silvery silk with its sparkling morning dew that looked like tiny diamonds. They stared at the spider and her web for a long time, before Claude brought Medea to a flowerbed, put her hand on a flower, and watched her smile as she felt the soft petals between her fingers.

After the twenty minutes were up, Ms. Rattlebee called them back together under the beech tree and invited them to tell each other about any experience that was particularly striking to them. There was silence for a while, but Ms. Rattlebee didn't seem at all fazed by the reluctance of the students to speak. She just waited.

Eventually, Medea spoke. "I watched a spider—this tiny, little being—create a perfect web. Her brain is so small, but she can do this extraordinary thing. And I had this realization that so many extraordinary things are happening all around us, all the time, if only we just paid attention."

After Medea broke the ice by speaking first, most of the other students had stories to share. The normally hard edge around Brent softened as he described smelling the soil that Lucas had lifted under his nose. He said that he'd never really appreciated that what he thought of as just dirt had such a strong and pleasant smell, and he had a sudden awareness of just how important soil is, and how it's different from sand and degraded dust, which barely smell at all and can't really grow anything.

Austin, who had been paired with Isaak, told the group how Isaak had brought him to a concrete area and had him kneel down before tapping his eye, and when he opened his eyes his initial thought was, "Why would Isaak show me a slab of concrete?"

"But then Isaak crouched down beside me and pointed to all the small plants growing in a crack in the concrete and tiny ants moving among them, and I was amazed that so many life forms find a way to live even in places that seem lifeless."

As each of them spoke, it was as if nature itself was speaking through them, telling its stories through their senses and awakening their curiosity and, indeed, their awe. Even Penelope and Will had positive experiences to share. Penelope spoke about seeing, and even hearing, the buzz of a bumblebee inside a flower and about noticing bright orange balls on the bee's legs. She said she wondered what the orange balls were and was going to find out when she got back to her computer.

When it was time to return to school, Ms. Rattlebee asked them to continue to walk in silence and to notice the sounds, sights, and smells. She invited them to consider all the forces in nature that made it possible for life to exist, including their own life.

Although they no longer had to, Claude and Medea continued to walk side by side.

At lunch, Medea was researching spiders on the Internet when she got a text from Claude asking whether she wanted to walk Rooper with him after school. With a math test coming up the next day, she texted back that she needed to study but hoped they could walk in the park with Rooper on Friday. "Sure," he wrote, realizing how disappointed he felt that she couldn't get together that afternoon. A week earlier, he didn't know a thing about Medea Ramon, and now he anticipated how much he would miss her that day. It was a little unsettling.

Walking home from school, Claude passed a dog tied to a parking meter. Lots of people tied their dogs to poles when they went inside stores to shop. Claude's parents taught him never to touch these dogs because they might bite, but sometimes Claude could just tell by the dogs' behaviors that they were going to be friendly, and occasionally he'd pet one. That's the kind of dog he saw, a small brown terrier with shaggy fur who wagged his tail furiously back and forth as soon as Claude smiled at him. The little dog wrinkled his nose into what looked like a grin and thumped his back leg as Claude scratched behind his ear. After a couple of minutes, Claude said goodbye to the dog and walked to the end of the block to a store where he bought some gum.

As he walked back out of the store, he heard a woman screaming.

"Where's my dog!? Where's Brady? Has anyone seen my dog? Help me!"

Claude ran over. The little brown dog he'd been petting was gone, and the woman was hysterical.

"I just saw your dog a few minutes ago! What happened?"

"I came out of the grocery store, and he was gone. Just gone. Oh no, where is he? Did you touch his leash?"

"No! Of course not!" Claude declared, horrified.

By now a crowd had gathered, and someone said they'd call the police. Claude backed away, unsure what to do to help the woman and upset that she thought he might have had anything to do with the disappearance of her dog.

Later that night, Farnsworth Cunningham came into Claude's room for their evening ritual. Farnsworth asked his son about his day, and Claude filled him in on classes and sports. Then, Claude asked his father about what was new in the world, and his dad said, "What? You mean you didn't watch the news!?" Then Farnsworth, who didn't really expect his twelve-year-old to watch him every night on TV, filled him in on the things he thought it was important for Claude to know.

Claude and his dad both enjoyed this time. It was, in fact, the only time they really talked. Farnsworth was never home for dinner on weeknights, and he spent the weekends playing golf in the warmer months, and racquetball in the winter. But it was during this time each weekday evening that Claude could count on his father paying attention to him, and he appreciated what he learned from him. His dad was very even and steady, always looked at things from many points of view, and never forced his opinions on Claude.

Tonight, Farnsworth started the conversation by saying, "Did you hear that there have been a couple of dogs stolen from the street? Make sure you don't tie Rooper out on a pole."

"Oh my gosh, Dad. I wanted to tell you about that! That happened today on Madison Avenue. A woman came out of a store, and her dog was gone. I'd seen the dog, too. His name was Brady, and he was really sweet."

"Yes, there have been a rash of these dog thefts, Claude. They reported it tonight on the local news. So be careful with Rooper."

CHAPTER 7

As Claude entered the seventh-grade classroom the next morning, Ms. Rattlebee was writing on the board. Her back was to the class, and she was wearing an extra-large T-shirt that went down to her knees. A few kids in the class (you can guess which ones) were laughing at a quote that covered the middle of Ms. Rattlebee's back. It read:

"MY LIFE IS MY MESSAGE"
—Mahatma Gandhi

Ms. Rattlebee turned around to address the class, and the laughing students tried very hard to contain themselves, especially when she immediately referred to the quote on her back.

"Some of you may have noticed Mahatma Gandhi's words on the back of my dress." (Penelope snorted at the word *dress*.) "Can any of you tell me what you think he meant when he said this?"

Medea raised her hand. "I think that he meant that what he did in his life was more important than what he said."

"Thank you, Medea. I think you're right. Mahatma Gandhi was a very great man who helped free India from British rule using only nonviolent methods. He was very famous and very revered, and one day a reporter asked him, 'What is your message for people?' Gandhi had taken a vow of silence that day, so even though he usually had a lot to say, he responded by jotting down on a piece of paper just five words: 'My life is my message.'

"None of us is Gandhi," Ms. Rattlebee continued, "but his quote is true for everybody. How each of us acts, how we treat others, what we do in the world—*that* is our message.

"Today is my last day with you. Mr. Bryant has recovered quite nicely and will be returning on Monday. I thought about what I wanted to do during our last class together, and I decided that the most important thing I had to teach you is that *your* life is *your* message. So, I'd like you to read the question I've written on the board and quietly write a response."

On the board, written in florid script, was this question:

Is your life the message you want it to be?

"I don't expect this assignment to be easy," Ms. Rattlebee said, "but I do expect you to write something. So, take out a piece of paper and get started. You have thirty minutes before I'll interrupt you. And don't worry. You can be completely honest, because no one is going to read what you write except you."

Thirty minutes! Few of the students had any idea how to answer such a strange question, and most were thinking,

"What on earth am I going to do for the next thirty minutes?" Once Will Wingfield heard that no one else would read what he wrote, he started drawing geometric shapes on his piece of paper, while Penelope began writing a list of gifts she wanted for Christmas. Claude, however, could feel his brain start buzzing again. This time, his body began to tremble, too. He was suddenly struck by the realization that his life was not really the message he wanted it to be. This is what he wrote:

> *I don't think my life is really the message I want it to be. I mean, before Ms. Rattlebee came to Worthington, I would've said it was. Well, I might not have understood the question really. But after what she's taught us, and now that Medea and I are talking about doing something to make a difference, I think I know what the question means. And I think I know what Gandhi meant because I've heard about him, and he really practiced what he preached.*
>
> *I haven't done much of anything for anyone. I mean I'm nice enough, but I haven't ever thought much about other people or animals or the environment, and I think if my life was really the message I wanted it to be, I'd be different. I'd do more for others. I wouldn't think only about myself. I guess becoming a vegetarian is part of making my life the message I want it to be, so that's good.*
>
> *I'm glad I met Medea. I hope she thinks her life is the message she wants it to be because she's*

pretty cool. I know this isn't supposed to be about Medea, but getting to know her makes me feel like my life is more the message I want it to be. That doesn't really make sense, but it's how I feel.

I wonder what everyone else is writing. I wonder what Austin thinks about his life. Or Will. Or Penelope. How could Penelope really think her life is the message she wants it to be? What could she be writing?

I don't think I'm supposed to be writing about the other kids. It really doesn't matter what they think about their life, or what they write. What matters is what I think about mine. And what I do with mine. So, what am I going to do? That's the big question.

I wish Ms. Rattlebee weren't leaving. I feel like telling her how much I've liked her classes, but I don't want anyone other than Medea to see me talking to her. Wow. That very thought is an example of not living my life as my message! I shouldn't care what others think of me if I believe in what I'm doing.

I don't know what else to write. I do want my life to be a better message than it's been so far. I think I can make it better. At least I can try.

Claude finished writing and looked up at the clock. It had been almost thirty minutes. He started to read over what he'd written when Ms. Rattlebee began talking to the class again.

"Okay, everyone. Time to finish up. I'm going to pass out envelopes. Please put your paper in an envelope, seal it, address it to yourself, and hand it back to me. Someday, when you least expect it, you'll receive it in the mail. When you do, open it up and read what you wrote. Notice what you think, and how you feel. Pay attention to whether you have made your life more the message you want it to be since writing what you did today."

The students did as Ms. Rattlebee asked, although it was clear that a couple of them did so reluctantly. Penelope was sneering as she shoved her Christmas wish list into an envelope, and Will looked irritated. But Claude stared at his self-addressed envelope, amazed by the changes that had taken place inside him. When he passed his envelope to Ms. Rattlebee, he looked into her eyes, feeling so much gratitude. She smiled at him and, as if she could read his mind, whispered, "You're quite welcome, Claude." Then she turned to the class.

"And now it's goodbye. I've written my email address and phone number on the board. If you ever want to contact me, please do. I hope that you'll think about all the ways you can make your one and only life the message you want it to be. There are a lot of things in the world that still need to be fixed, and who better than you?" And at that, she picked up her giant patchwork bag, turned on her small feet, and walked out of the room.

Claude was filled with sadness. Ms. Rattlebee was the most bizarre person he'd ever encountered. She was the shortest grown-up he'd ever met, with the highest voice he'd ever heard, and the strangest clothes he'd ever seen. But she was also the most unique, original, and interesting teacher he'd ever had. The five mornings he'd spent with her were the most important and memorable of all the mornings in all the years he'd been at school. He wondered for a moment if he would simply turn back into the Claude who was so familiar to him—the one who didn't have many cares in the world and was definitely not trying to figure out how to save it. But then he thought about what he'd just written, and he understood it was too late to go back to being that Claude. He knew he had to do something that mattered.

Claude was in a funk for most of the rest of the day. The only thing that lifted his spirits was remembering that he and Medea would be getting Rooper and walking in the park after school. Knowing that he would have her to talk to brightened his spirits.

When they were in the park, Claude told Medea all about Brady, the little brown dog he'd met the day before, and about his conversation with his dad.

"That's it, Claude! That's what we'll do. We're going to get to the bottom of these dog thefts and stop them!"

"What?! Are you crazy, Medea? It's one thing to learn about what's happening in the world and try to do something about it, and it's another thing to become detectives in our spare time and stop criminals from stealing dogs. I thought you had to stay out of trouble. What makes you think the police won't find out who's stealing the dogs?"

"Claude, remember what Ms. Rattlebee said when she pretended to be the alien Grinwhistle? People let all sorts of horrible things happen to animals. Do you think the dognappings are a high priority for the police?"

"Okay, maybe that's true, but what do you think we should do?"

"We can watch the dogs who are tied up on the street and find out who's taking them, that's what. It would be better if we split up, though, so we can watch more dogs. How about we start tomorrow afternoon, since it's Saturday and we'll have more time? That is, if you're free." Medea suddenly seemed shy and uncertain.

"Sure, I can meet tomorrow," Claude said, since he'd be done with his violin lesson in the morning.

"Excellent. Let's meet at noon. How about 86th and Madison? I don't think you should bring Rooper." (Rooper looked up expectantly at the sound of his name, but realized it wasn't good news for him and dropped his head.)

Chapter 8

The next day, Claude and Medea met as planned. They split up on Madison Avenue, each planning to walk until they saw a dog tied to a pole and then watch as discreetly as possible. They agreed to check in periodically and to report any suspicious activities to each other.

After a few hours, nothing had happened. Claude had watched a little terrier (who looked just like Toto in *The Wizard of Oz*); a black lab; two whippets; a black-and-white, long-haired dog; a dog who looked like a miniature German shepherd; and a fluffy puppy. Medea had watched the same dog for a long time. She was a tiny, nervous pup who shook practically the whole time, staring at the spot where her guardian had disappeared into a clothing store for an hour. The dog looked so scared and vulnerable tied to the pole, and Medea wondered what it must be like to have people zooming by you and almost stepping on you. After the dog's guardian finally came out, she was so excited she peed all over the place. Watching her made Medea sad. She walked a few more blocks looking for other dogs, watched a couple more, and then checked in with Claude.

"Nothing at this end," she said.

"Me neither. Shall we call it quits for today?"

They met back at 86th Street, feeling a bit discouraged. They had been so enthusiastic about their mission, and now it appeared that it was going to be harder than they imagined to stop the dog thefts. But they were determined to try again. Medea said she couldn't do it on Sunday, because she always spent Sundays with her dad, but that she could meet again after school on Monday.

Claude walked home, greeted Rooper, and took him on his promised walk in the park. He paid extra attention to him and stopped periodically just to hug his beautiful best friend. Watching all the dogs that afternoon made him realize just how much these animals depended upon their humans. All the dogs looked so forlorn when they were tied up, and some looked downright scared. He would never let Rooper feel that way.

As they walked through Central Park, Claude realized how much more he was noticing than usual: the rustle of leaves in the wind, the fat-cheeked chipmunks, the cooing pigeons bobbing their heads as they walked along the paths looking for crumbs to eat; even the warmth of the sun on his face. He could feel that same tingling joy that he'd experienced during the Wonder Walk. When his eyes met those of an elderly man who was sitting on a bench, and the man broke out into a big smile, Claude suddenly felt that he got a glimpse of what it meant to live his message the way he wanted.

Medea walked home, too. Usually, she spent part of Saturday afternoons with her neighborhood friends at a skate park.

She was an awesome skateboarder, the best in the group, which was saying a lot because they were all skateboarders. There was a playground that had fallen into disrepair a few blocks from her apartment building, and the kids had turned it into one of the best skate parks in Manhattan. They had created ramps and different jumps using the old seesaws and concrete tunnels, and skateboarders from all over East Harlem came to practice their skills and hang out together. Medea was still feeling discouraged about their lack of success at finding the dognappers, and she wasn't in the mood to hang out with her friends. She decided to just go upstairs to her apartment.

Marvin was in the kitchen preparing dinner.

"Hi, Dad."

"Hi, sweetheart." Marvin smiled when he saw his beloved daughter. "You hungry?"

"A little. Can I help?" Medea asked as she walked into the kitchen and hugged her dad.

"Sure. How about you mash the avocados? We're having tacos with beans, rice, salsa, and guacamole and a big salad. How was your day?"

"It was good," Medea replied, pausing to decide whether to tell him about Claude, since her dad always worried that she had no friends at school. "I sort of have a new friend. In fact, we're probably going to hang out after school most days next week, okay?" Medea decided not to mention her new friend's name because she wasn't sure what her dad would think or say if he knew this friend was Claude Maxwell-Cunningham, a boy he opened doors for at work.

Marvin sensed she didn't want to divulge more, so he didn't probe. He just said, "Of course, sweetheart. I'm so glad you've made a friend at school."

While Medea was cooking dinner with her dad, Claude had joined Marisa in the kitchen to watch the local news. Since this was unusual behavior for Claude, Marisa couldn't help but ask, "To what do I owe the pleasure of your company, Claude? A local sports team on the news tonight?"

"No, Marisa. It's not that. I wanted to find out what was going on with the dognappings. I saw a dog when I was coming home from school this past week. He was stolen while I was in a store. I'd pet him and everything. Dad said there was a story on the news about it. So, I want to see if anything else happened today."

Right at the beginning of the news, when the newscaster reported the headlines before breaking for a commercial, he announced: "Coming up: another Manhattan dognapping."

"Holy cow!" Claude exclaimed and quickly texted Medea to turn on the news.

"Who are you texting, Claude?"

"Oh, a friend is also interested in the dognappings. I wanted to let her know to watch the news."

Marisa wasn't quite sure what to make of Claude's behavior, which was decidedly odd, but before she had time to give his strange actions more thought, the news was back on.

Claude couldn't believe it. A dog had been stolen on 82nd and Third that afternoon. He had only been two blocks away! The newscaster encouraged people to keep their dogs by their sides at all times, and then the news shifted to other events.

"Excuse me, Marisa. I'll see you later," Claude said as he dashed out again. Marisa watched him leave, wondering what was going on inside the normally even-tempered Claude. She decided she would have to watch him more closely.

Claude called Medea right away.

"Did you watch it?"

"Yes! Listen, Claude, we're going to need more help. I can probably get some friends from my neighborhood to come on Monday. With all the news reports, the dognappings probably aren't going to continue much longer, at least not in your neighborhood. We may only have a few more days to find out who's stealing the dogs."

"That sounds good. I'll see you on Monday. Bye, Medea."

Medea told her dad she was going to go outside to the skate park briefly before dinner. She grabbed her skateboard and dashed out. When she got to the park, she was greeted with a warm welcome from her friends.

"Hey Medea, where've you been? We've been missing our genius queen of the park." This came from Hector, a thirteen-year-old boy who was almost as good a skateboarder as Medea, and who was the unofficial leader of the group.

"Hector, I need your help," Medea quietly said to him.

"Anything, girl. You know it," Hector replied, and Medea filled him in on what was happening.

Hector called to the other skateboarders, and they came over to see what was going on. Medea filled them in, and they agreed to meet on Monday afternoon to help.

Chapter 9

At 3:30 p.m. on Monday, eight children gathered on 86th and Madison. Medea introduced her friends to Claude, who had brought his skateboard as well. Along with Hector, there was Rodney, Analena, Monique, Pedro, and Leon. Then, Medea assigned streets and avenues for patrol, and the kids dispersed in pairs.

One hour later, Rodney texted the group:

> Van parked by hydrant 90th & Lex. One guy in van.
> Big, bald guy walking toward dog tied up by store.
> Oh no, he's already grabbed the dog! Gotta go!

Rodney didn't know what he should do, so he did what came naturally—hopped on his skateboard. He zoomed down the street toward the man and the dog, but the man saw him coming and jumped out of the way just as Rodney was about to crash into him. The man called out, "Stupid punk," and walked as quickly as he could toward the van.

By the time the other kids had converged on the block, the van was long gone, but Rodney had noted the van's color and make and had noticed it had a New Jersey license plate, but he hadn't been quick enough to take a photo with his phone. Everyone wanted to know the details of the dognapping, and Rodney was quick to tell them.

"The guy was huge and had these doughy jowls and freaky, little eyes. He walked like a sumo wrestler, sort of rocking from side to side. He was scary, man. There wasn't anything I could do to stop him. I tried crashing into him on my skateboard, but he got out of the way. Man, I wish I could've stopped him."

"It's not your fault, Rodney," Medea reassured him. "It's great that you know what he looks like, and now we have information about the van."

The kids didn't know quite what to say or do, and there was an awkward silence as they stood on the street wondering what should happen next. Finally, Hector spoke up.

"We need to get a phone in the van to record what's happening and track where it goes. We gotta know why they're stealing the dogs, and what they're doing to them."

Claude and Medea looked at each other, both thinking the same thing: *What have we gotten ourselves into?* Like Hector, they wanted to get to the bottom of this, but wasn't that a job for the police? The news was already reporting the dognappings. Shouldn't they just go to the authorities and tell them about the men in the van? But when Claude expressed this out loud, Hector just laughed.

"You think the police are going to listen to us? A bunch of kids from East Harlem? The police spend all their time busting us for hanging out in the park after it gets dark."

Claude didn't feel like telling Medea's friends where he lived, or that his mother was their senator and his father was on TV every night reporting the national news.

When Claude got home, their plan began to seem more and more risky. He decided to call Medea, figuring that together they'd come to their senses.

"Hey Medea, I've been thinking ... " he began.

"You're getting cold feet, aren't you?" she interrupted, with a judgmental edge to her voice.

"I just think we should let the police handle this. I mean, how are we going to get a phone in the van? And what are we going to do then? Follow the van? Isn't this getting kind of out of hand?"

There was a long pause on the phone.

"I don't think we should give up so soon, Claude. I don't know if the police will really catch these guys. There are a lot of white vans with New Jersey plates in Manhattan." Medea paused again, and Claude found himself fidgeting on the other end of the phone. Finally, she spoke, and her voice sounded like her mind was made up. "We can ask José for his help."

"Who's José?"

"He's Analena's older brother. He's in his twenties. He and Analena came here a couple of years ago from Puerto Rico, and they live around the corner from me. José is a housepainter, and he has a truck for his business. Since we'll need to follow the van once we have a phone in it, we can ask José if he'll drive his truck. I think José is the kind of guy who would want to help out."

"Medea, don't you think this is getting a little crazy? I can't just follow criminals with some guy I don't even know."

"I just told you José is Analena's brother. You know Analena."

"I just met her today, for crying out loud. My parents would kill me if they knew what we were planning. Aren't you worried about getting caught?"

Medea paused again. "Well . . . yes. But this is important, Claude. Don't you want to find that little dog, Brady? Don't you want to *do* something?"

Claude felt like Medea was accusing him of not caring enough. He was looking at Rooper while she spoke and found himself feeling a combination of guilt, cowardice, and, if he was honest, defensiveness.

"Yes, I want to *do* something," he snapped. "But this is what the police are for! Calling the police *is* doing something!"

There was silence on the phone.

"I need time to think," he said more quietly. "I'll see you tomorrow at school." And then he hung up and lay down on the floor with Rooper, confused, overwhelmed, and upset that he'd snapped at Medea.

Claude had trouble focusing on his homework that night, and when he went to bed, he couldn't fall asleep for a long time. His thoughts were spinning. What if Hector was right and the police didn't do anything? Could he live with himself if Brady and the other stolen dogs suffered some terrible fate? And how was it that Medea and her friends were so courageous, while he was having second thoughts about taking any risks? Medea had a lot more to lose if she got caught by the police. No matter how angry they'd be, Claude's parents would be able to protect him from any serious repercussions, but what would happen to Medea? What would happen to her friends? Was he being wise or just being a coward?

When he finally fell asleep, he dreamt that he was at a big outdoor pool with a high diving board. Kids were diving off the board, and he decided he wanted to dive, too. But as he started to climb up the ladder, it kept getting longer and longer until, when he finally got to the top, he was high up in the air. The pool was way down below him, and he was terrified.

He could barely see the kids in the pool, but he could hear them shouting, "Stop being a coward!" He stood on the board, paralyzed with fear, and he realized that he just wanted to get off that board, and he didn't want to jump. If kids were going to jeer at him, so be it.

He carefully turned around to go back to the ladder and climb down, but when he got to where the ladder was supposed to be, it was gone, and the diving board started rising again. Then he heard a dog bark and turned back around. Brady was standing on the other end of the diving board, right at the edge. Claude got down on his hands and knees to crawl to the little dog. But just as he reached him, Brady backed away and started to slip off the board. Claude reached out to save him, but he was too late. Brady tumbled down toward the pool, and Claude lost his balance and fell down behind him.

Claude awoke with a gasp, his heart racing.

For a long time, he couldn't fall back asleep. He kept thinking about the nightmare he'd just had. He had tried to save Brady in his dream. It was now clear to him that he would try to save him in reality. Even though it was the middle of the night, he texted Medea before he could lose his nerve.

"Okay. Let's save Brady. We can make a plan after school."

Chapter 10

The next day at school, Claude and Medea were both feeling a combination of loss and anxiety. They missed Ms. Rattlebee, and they were also worried about the path on which they were about to embark. Without Ms. Rattlebee, school felt irrelevant, and they had trouble concentrating on their classes. Both also felt short-tempered with some of their classmates. Medea was used to ignoring Penelope and her crowd, but when Penelope kept gushing to Mr. Bryant that she was so relieved that he was well and teaching their class after such a trying week with that "Rattlebee woman," Medea found herself seething. Meanwhile, Claude realized he couldn't care less about the various topics of conversation that captivated Austin, Tony, and Will at lunch.

What wasn't similar was their thinking about their plans to catch the dognappers. While Claude had discovered his own resolve, it was Medea's turn to have cold feet. They needed time together to talk, and they were both just waiting for school to be over so that they could walk Rooper in the park.

As they walked together after school, Claude listened to Medea express her growing doubts and fears. She talked about not being able to concentrate in class. She said she was worried that what had always been the most important things to her—learning, studying, doing well in school, and not getting in trouble—were hardly important at all anymore. She remarked that all she could think about were the stolen dogs and the dognappers, and she just wanted to go back in time and become normal Medea again. "But," she said, "then I think about Ms. Rattlebee, and I want to be brave and do something important."

After he had listened to Medea talk and understood exactly how she felt, Claude decided it was his turn to share what was going on inside of him. He told Medea about his nightmare and about how, in the midst of his terror, he discovered he had courage that he didn't know he had. He said he thought it was Medea's bravery that had rubbed off on him, and that her conviction the day before was who she really was, deep inside.

"Is it even possible that we could go back to who we were before Ms. Rattlebee?" he asked Medea.

Medea sighed. "Probably not. But I'm scared, Claude."

"Me, too. But my guess is that Brady and the other dogs are even more scared."

Over the next hour, they made a plan. Medea would talk to her friends about meeting again the next afternoon after school. They'd fan out and find the van and the dognappers. Claude would sneak into the van, video call Medea, leave his phone in the van to record what was happening, slip out, and then they'd follow the van in José's car. If they lost the van, they'd still be able to track Claude's phone.

Before they said goodbye, they looked into each other's eyes with resolve, trying to give each other a dose of bravery. Then Medea crouched down, wrapped her arms around Rooper, and buried her head behind his soft ear to give him a kiss. Claude felt a wave of emotion watching her do this, and he didn't quite know what to make of it. He pushed his feelings out of his mind as she stood up, smiled at him, and said, "See you tomorrow, Claude."

Before he went to bed that night, Claude took care of the remaining details. He asked his dad if he could stay at a friend's house the next night. Farnsworth was so exhausted after what had been a very long day that he didn't even ask Claude which friend's house; he just said that was fine. Claude put a change of clothes and his toothbrush in his backpack, plugged his phone in to make sure it was fully charged for the next day, and went to sleep earlier than usual.

Meanwhile, Medea asked her dad if she could spend the next night at Analena's. Marvin was always happy to have Medea sleep over at a friend's house since he was working all night, and he replied, "Of course, sweetie."

Chapter 11

The next day after school, the group of kids—along with José—met again on 86th and Madison. Claude and José introduced themselves to each other, and they went over their plan. They would pair up again, but this time they'd be looking for the van, not just dogs tied to poles. They'd cover ground on their skateboards, and José would drive up and down the avenues in his truck. As soon as someone spotted the van, they'd contact the rest of the group and then convene at that location.

Once they had the van in sight, the plan was to distract the guy who was approaching the dog, make enough of a commotion that the other guy would also come out of the van, and while the two men were out of the vehicle, Claude would sneak in and hide his phone, having called Medea, who would then keep her phone on mute so that they could listen and watch what was happening in the van without being heard. Then, Medea, Analena, and Claude would get in the truck with José, and they'd follow the van and use another phone to tape what they were hearing and seeing on Medea's phone. They'd get Claude's phone back once the van got to its destination.

Two hours later, Monique Martin, who was the fastest of the skateboarders, spotted a white van with New Jersey plates in front of Bloomingdales on Lexington and 59th Street and contacted the group. There was a small Pomeranian tied in front of the store, and knowing how fast the guy from the van could steal a dog, Monique quickly skateboarded over. A big man who fit the description from Rodney was already approaching the dog. They got to her at the same time.

"Oh, look how cute!" Monique exclaimed and started petting her. "Is she yours?" she asked, staring into the man's jowly face to get a good look at him.

"Yeah, kid. But sometimes she bites, so you should probably back off."

"Oh, she seems so friendly. What's her name?"

"Uh, Spot," he answered.

"Spot! That's funny. She doesn't have any spots. How did you come up with that name?"

By now, the others had begun to congregate. Luckily, José had been just around the corner when Monique contacted them, and he was now idling his truck in front of a hydrant about a hundred feet behind the van. Claude threw his skateboard in the back of the truck and called Medea so that his phone would be ready to record what was happening. Medea answered the call, muted her phone, turned off the sound, and then joined her friends around the little dog. They all started "oohing" and "aahing" over "Spot."

"Let *me* pet her," yelled Hector from behind the other kids as he shoved his way through the group.

"Uh, I'd like you kids to leave her alone now. We gotta get going."

Monique was bending over "Spot" and examining her tag.

"This is strange," she said. "It says on her tag that her name is Luna, and that her guardian is Joanna Pomfrey. I thought this was your dog."

The man stared at Monique menacingly. "Get away from my dog, kid. *Now.*"

It looked like their plan was going to fail. The other guy hadn't come out of the van, which meant that Claude hadn't been able to get his phone in the van. The man seemed dangerous, and they knew they couldn't keep this up.

Then Medea suddenly cried, "Ow! Your dog bit me!" She clutched her "bitten" hand, curled over on the sidewalk, and started pretending to sob. This was finally enough to get the other guy to come out of the van to see what was going on.

As Medea lay doubled over on the street crying and moaning, Claude ran over to the van, opened the door and got in. He climbed over the front seats, and discovered four cages, three of which had dogs in them, all strangely subdued.

"Oh no," he whispered. "I've got to get you guys out of here." But then he thought about their plan and wondered if he'd have enough time to get the dogs out and whether documenting what was happening and finding out where the dogs were going would help more. He knew he only had moments to decide.

"I'm sorry, but I've got to make sure these guys get caught," he said to the dogs as he looked around for a place to put his phone so that it would be both hidden and able to record what was happening. There was such a mess and jumble that it was unlikely that the men would find the phone, which he decided to secure to a tall cage near the top of the van. All of a sudden, he heard Medea screeching into the phone.

"They're coming, Claude! Get out of there! They'll be opening the door in about twenty seconds!"

Claude hadn't been able to get his phone in position yet, but even worse, he had no time to get out of the van. If he'd tried to slip out either front door, he'd be seen, and there was no way he could climb over all the cages and exit through the rear door quickly enough. He was trapped. He used the remaining seconds to hide himself between the front seat and the cages.

The front doors of the van opened, and the two men climbed in. The driver turned the ignition key, swerved out, and took off.

Claude's heart was pounding so loudly he was sure the men would be able to hear it. He knew he needed to slow his breathing down and stay calm and quiet. He carefully lifted his phone so that he would capture the men on video, and so Medea could see what was happening. Surely, she'd call the police now. But then he realized what would happen if she did. Claude's parents would find out what he'd been up to, and they'd be furious. They'd never trust him again. He began hoping she wouldn't call the police. He'd get out of this somehow.

As his breathing slowed, he started listening to the men screaming at each other.

"You idiot! What did you think you were doin' talking to those kids! You shoulda just left, and we coulda found another dog. They saw you. They're suspicious."

"Calm down, Mack. They're just a bunch of kids. If the old lady hadn't come out and asked us what we were all doing with her dog, it would've been fine. That dog was perfect for us—small, easy to grab—just what Hellburn's looking for."

"No mutt is worth gettin' caught, Haskell! Don't be so stupid, you stupid, imbecilic idiot."

"Okay, okay, I'm sorry. Just calm down, Mack. We still need to get one more dog before the day is out. Let's head to Gristedes on 75th Street. People always spend a lot of time there. Let's see if there's a dog out front."

Claude prayed that José was following, and that Medea was watching, but even if they were, what could they do? He just hoped they would think of something. Then the van came to a stop, and Haskell got out to find another dog. A minute later, he opened the back of the van and roughly stuffed a little beagle into the empty cage and injected the dog with something from a hypodermic needle. That explained why the dogs were so calm, Claude realized—they were drugged.

Claude could barely breathe, he was so terrified. If Haskell had looked up when he'd put the dog in the van, he would have seen Claude. Fortunately, there was a big cage with a good-sized Samoyed in it. The dog was quite fluffy, and that helped to keep Claude hidden.

Haskell got back into the van, and Mack muttered, "All right, you redeemed yourself. We're done for the day. Let's get something to eat on our way to Hellburn."

A few minutes later, Mack started screaming again.

"Look at this traffic! It's gonna take us an hour to get through the tunnel. I hate New York and the stinkin' traffic!"

Mack started honking his horn repeatedly.

"Calm down, Mack. Let's just be cool and quiet, okay? We've got a van full of stolen dogs. Let's not tick anyone off. Look, the traffic's moving. It won't take so long."

Thirty minutes later, the van came to a stop, and Mack and Haskell got out. Waiting a minute until he felt sure they were out of sight, Claude crept out. The van was parked at a Denny's in a strip mall in New Jersey.

Claude quickly ran in the opposite direction of Denny's, putting some distance between himself and the two men. Unsure of what he should do next, he waited and watched. A moment later, he saw José's truck pull into the parking lot. He ran over.

Medea rolled down the window and called to Claude, "Hurry! Get in."

Claude opened the door and climbed in. He started filling them in on what had happened, but then heard his voice coming out of Medea's phone.

"Oh, no!" Claude cried. "I have my phone. I have to go back and leave it in the van!"

"Don't be crazy, Claude. We'll just follow the van. We've got enough evidence already. It's too dangerous. I was terrified with you in that van!"

Claude smiled at Medea. He liked that she'd been so worried about him, and somehow the fact that she cared so much made him want to be even braver.

"I've got to go back there, Medea. We don't know anything yet, except that some guy named Hellburn wants these dogs. And what if we lose them in the traffic? I'll tape my phone to the big cage and come right back."

Claude ran to the van and got back in.

He spoke softly to the dogs.

"It'll be okay, guys. I'm going to get you out of here. I promise."

But just as he'd gotten his phone secured to the cage and angled toward the front, Mack and Haskell came back. They'd gotten takeout food instead of eating at the restaurant, which meant that Claude was stuck in the van again.

The men started talking about where they might hit next.

"New York is getting too dicey with the news reports. How 'bout Philadelphia? It's quieted down, doncha think?"

"I dunno. There was an awful lot of publicity about us eight months ago. It might be too soon." Mack sounded proud.

"But we gotta keep the dogs comin'. Hellburn just gets more and more business."

"Yeah, Hellburn's sure gotta good racket goin' on. Not too many research institutes are willing to make the studies come out just the way the companies want them," Mack said, and chuckled.

"Yeah, I gotta hand it to Hellburn; he's gotta good gig with those toxilogical studies."

"You idiot, it's toxicological, not toxilogical!"

"Whatever." Haskell paused, before adding, "What exactly does that mean, anyway?"

"What a lame excuse for a human being you are, Haskell. The Hellburn Research Institute does studies on chemicals. *Toxicological* studies. *Poison* studies. That's what the dogs are for, you idiot. To test the chemicals."

"But I thought that Hellburn's research helped protect companies from lawsuits."

"They do, you imbecile. They write up the dog studies just right to show what the companies want them to show. I can't talk to you anymore. You're too stupid for words."

Chapter 12

Fifteen minutes later, the van pulled up to a gate with a guard out front. Claude heard Mack say, "We got the dogs."

"Back into the shed, then. I hope you got a good batch this time. Hellburn complained you're bringing too many big ones, and he's not happy about the TV reports."

Mack backed the van into a garage-like shed attached to the main building, and then he and Haskell got out. They opened the back door of the van, and Claude heard Mack yell, "Aw, man, this one dumped in his cage, and he's covered in it. You grab him, Haskell. I'm gonna be sick. It stinks in here, you worthless bag of fleas."

With all the commotion, Claude was able to get his phone, climb into the front of the van unnoticed, and crouch down out of sight. Although he couldn't see anyone, he could still hear what was going on outside the van, and he hoped Medea could, too. Once Mack and Haskell had removed all of the dogs, Claude heard Mack say, "Okay Haskell, let's get 'em to the dog room before the drugs wear off."

Then, a moment later, his voice full of fear, Mack stuttered, "Oh, g-g-good evening, Dr. Hellburn. We got a good b-b-batch for you. We were just gonna take them to Room 101."

"What's that Samoyed doing here, Mack?" Dr. Hellburn was pointing at the big, white dog. His voice was controlled, but Claude thought he sounded furious. And dangerous.

"Oh, we're very sorry, Dr. Hellburn. She was so easy to get, so friendly and all. She's really not that b-b-big. It's mostly fluff on her."

"She's a big dog, Mack, and I've told you no big dogs. Big dogs eat a lot of food and take up a lot of space and give me a hard time." Dr. Hellburn sounded like he was trying to explain something very simple to a child he thought was very dumb. He also sounded like he might punish that child very badly. "I don't like it when you disobey me, Mack."

"Okay, Dr. Hellburn. It won't happen again, sir." Mack sounded terrified.

"No, I'm sure it won't."

Then, Dr. Hellburn growled, "Take them down the hall and put them in cages. And prepare Number 3 for the arsenic test. Let's prove once and for all that a bit of arsenic in our water isn't so dangerous, shall we?" Dr. Hellburn was chuckling to himself as he walked back into the building.

Mack and Haskell dragged the dogs into the building. They were now almost fully awake, and some pulled at their leashes. Mack had to struggle especially hard with the big Samoyed. As the door to the building was closing behind Mack, Claude heard him yelling, "Get over here, you filthy animal, or I'll break your neck."

Claude slipped out of the van, hiding behind a row of boxes in the shed. He was afraid to walk into the building until Mack and Haskell were gone, and he figured they'd probably come back to their truck when they were done unloading the dogs and preparing Number 3 for the arsenic test, whatever that meant.

Back in the truck, José, Analena, and Medea had heard Mack speak to the guard at the gate before entering the research lab. As they wound their way down the driveway toward the gate, they realized they had no idea how they would get past the guard. José pulled over so that they could come up with a plan. He and Analena started talking out loud, trying to figure out a way to get in, until Medea shushed them. She was busy trying to hear what was going on in the shed while continuing to record everything with José's phone. She could just barely hear the exchange between Mack and Dr. Hellburn. After Mack and Haskell had dragged the dogs into the building and no one was speaking on the phone, she turned her attention to the task of getting past the guard.

Whenever Medea needed to solve a problem, she got a faraway look in her eyes as she seemed to disappear deep inside her own mind. After several minutes of this intense concentration, she had come up with a solution. Her idea was a gamble, but she thought it was their best hope. She explained the plan to José and Analena, who hadn't come up with anything better.

Medea and Analena climbed in the back of the truck, and José covered them up with the drop cloths he used in his painting business, putting heavy paint cans on the edges to make it look like he was securing what was under the cloth. Medea and Analena balled themselves up, pretending to be dogs in crates. The guard came out and eyed José suspiciously.

"Who are *you*?"

"Juan Diaz," answered José (who didn't want to give his real name, of course). I'm doing work for Mack and Haskell. They told me Dr. Hellburn wanted some more animals. I got a few little doggies in the back. They said to get 'em here quick."

"How come I don't know you?"

"Mack and Haskell just brought me on today. They said they needed help because Dr. Hellburn wanted more dogs than they could get themselves. Please, man, I don't want to get in any trouble with Mack, you know?"

The guard opened the gate. "Okay, go to the shed up ahead. Mack and Haskell just came in with their truck. You should see them there."

Moments later, Medea heard voices coming out of her phone again. Mack and Haskell had come back into the shed, and she heard Mack say, "We're outta here, Haskell. Let's go home."

What Medea couldn't hear was what happened as the van approached the gate to leave. The guard motioned to Mack and Haskell to stop. Haskell rolled down the window, and the guard smirked. "Got a new associate, huh? Can't do the job yourselves?"

Mack and Haskell exchanged glances.

"Whatchyoo talkin' about? We don't need no help," Haskell replied.

"No? Well, your new friend Juan just came in with more dogs. Said Hellburn wanted more than the two of you were bringing him. Didn't you see them?"

Mack was too angry to speak. He gave the guard a baleful look, floored the accelerator, and zoomed off. "That's the kind of treatment we get after stealin' dogs for him for all these years! I'm gonna have a talk with the doctor," Mack blustered.

"I don't get it. You really think Hellburn hired someone else?"

"I don't care, Haskell. I'm going home. If he did hire someone else, he's welcome to him. I bring Hellburn a nice bunch of dogs, and he yells at me about their size and hires someone else. That's the thanks we get for doin' his dirty work."

Back in the shed, Claude slipped out from where he'd been hiding and slowly opened the door to the building. Moments later, José drove the truck into the shed. Since they didn't see Claude anywhere, they thought it would be best to hold tight and wait for him to speak.

They didn't have to wait long.

"Medea," Claude whispered. "Are you there?"

Medea unmuted her phone, so relieved to hear Claude's voice.

"Yes, Claude. We're here," she whispered back. "We are parked in the shed where the van was. Where are you?"

"I'm in the building," he whispered, holding up his phone to show them what he was seeing. "But my phone is almost dead. I'm going to hang up to save the battery. I'll text you."

"Wait, Claude!" Medea exclaimed as quietly as she could, but it was too late. He had hung up, and while she wanted to call him back, she didn't want his phone to die when he might need it most.

Claude found himself in a sterile-looking hallway with white linoleum floors and white walls. Although it looked a bit like a hospital, it was the creepiest place he'd ever been, which was weird since there was nothing obviously horrible about it. There was a strong smell of chemicals that made him feel sick and fluorescent lights that turned his skin faintly green. Aside from an irritating buzzing sound that came from the lights, the building was completely silent. But it was not a peaceful silence and Claude had a terrible foreboding that when the silence was broken, it would be by crying animals.

The building seemed deserted, which made sense because it was after business hours and most of the employees would have gone home. As he walked down the hallway, he came to a door with a sign in front that read ROOM 105: TESTING LABORATORY. He pressed his ear to the door and listened. All was quiet. Despite the dying battery on his phone, he knew it would be a good idea to document what he was seeing, so he turned his phone back on and started videotaping.

Inside the testing lab were stainless steel tables with big metal devices that had shackles on them. Claude didn't know exactly what they were for, but it looked like they were built to hold animals in place. There were lots of cabinets, and Claude opened one up to see what was inside. It was filled with bottles of chemicals, some of which said

POISON on them. There was even one that had a skull and crossbones on the label. Claude videotaped everything in the room before quietly going back to the hallway.

The sign in front of the next room read 101: DOG ROOM. Again, Claude pressed his ear to the door to make sure no one was inside before he slowly opened it. The room was full of cages, seven of which had dogs inside them. The ones from the van looked up at Claude, and a couple of them started barking, while the others shuffled back to the corners of their cages and began to shake.

"Shhh, you guys. Please stay quiet," Claude whispered. "I promise I won't hurt you."

One of the trembling dogs was Brady, the little terrier who had been stolen the previous week. On his cage was a white card with the number 3 written with a thick marker.

There was also a cage on the floor that didn't seem to belong there. It was a tiny plastic box, smaller than a shoebox, with a white rat crammed inside it.

Claude videotaped the animals in their cages, and then became aware that it was time to actually save them. But just then, Claude heard footsteps, and quickly hid behind some cages where he could still see and videotape what was happening in the room.

Dr. Hellburn walked in. Claude knew it was him because his white lab coat had "Dr. Harcourt Hellburn, President" stitched onto the pocket. He was very tall, with short-cropped blond hair and a long, pale face with barely any lips at all—just an angry, flat line in the huge space between his nose and his chin. He had a nasty, cruel look about him that made Claude shudder.

Dr. Hellburn opened the cage that Brady was in and took the little dog out by the scruff of his neck. Claude had never seen a dog look so terrified. Brady started yelping and struggling, and Dr. Hellburn squeezed him harder.

"Shut up, mongrel," he hissed. "It's time to earn your dog chow. You must be thirsty for some arsenic-laced water, eh? Don't worry, you'll still be alive tonight, but I hope you didn't have any big plans for next week." Dr. Hellburn was cackling as he left the room with the little dog.

About ten minutes later, Dr. Hellburn walked back in, threw Brady roughly into his cage and slammed the cage door, chortling, "Sleep tight, mongrel."

As Dr. Hellburn turned to leave the room, he tripped over the plastic box with the rat in it.

"What the . . . !" he shouted. "What are you doing here? Mack is going to be very sorry that he's not more careful with the test subjects. Well, you can just stay here tonight and listen to the dogs bark until Mack puts you back where you belong in the morning," he yelled at the rat, before kicking the box and striding out of the room.

Claude had gotten the whole scene on video, and he quickly texted it to Medea just before his phone died. Then, he scooted over to Brady, who was trembling and looked weak. He opened the cage and picked up the little dog, holding him close to his body. "I'll get you out of here, Brady. I promise."

After watching the scene in Room 101, Medea was frantic. She was terrified that Dr. Hellburn would catch Claude, and she knew they needed to go help him with the dogs.

They crept out of the truck, waited a minute until they felt confident the coast was clear, and opened the door to the building. They looked down the empty hallway, then quickly but quietly walked toward Room 101. Medea shivered. The antiseptic smell made her sick to her stomach, too, and she had the same creepy feeling that Claude had had when he had entered the building.

There it was, 101: DOG ROOM. Medea opened the door and saw Claude holding Brady. The dog looked awful and was still shaking all over.

"Thank goodness! Let's get the dogs out of here," she whispered.

There were leashes hanging from a hook, and Medea, José, and Analena each took two dogs, while Claude carried Brady in his arms. Fortunately, the dogs stayed quiet, perhaps sensing that the purposeful hush of their rescuers was a sign to be silent, too. They led the dogs to José's truck and carefully lifted each one into the back. Claude, Medea, and Analena were about to climb under the drop cloth with the dogs when Claude remembered the rat who was in the plastic box on the floor of the dog room. "Wait! I've got to go back and get that rat out of there!"

José looked at Claude like he was crazy. "You're going to save a rat?! Let's just get out of here, Claude. The guy at the gate might start to wonder where we are. Or Hellburn could come back any second. I want to help you guys, but don't be nuts, man. I'm not willing to risk getting caught for a rat!"

But Claude had looked into the rat's eyes and had seen a suffering animal not so different from the dogs. He couldn't leave without trying to rescue her, too.

"Sorry, José, but I've got to. I'll be right back." And Claude dashed out before José could say anything more.

The coast was still clear. Claude sprinted to Room 101 and grabbed the box with the rat. But as he walked back into the hallway, he came face to face with a strange-looking woman whose skin looked as if it had been stretched really tightly across her bones.

"Who are you? And what are you doing with that rat?" she asked in a nasal voice that sounded like it came out of a machine instead of a person.

"Um, I'm Jason. I'm Dr. Hellburn's nephew," responded Claude, thinking quickly. "I'm helping out. Harcourt asked me to put the rat back where it belongs. It was left in the dog room by mistake." Claude thought that if he used Dr. Hellburn's first name, the woman would be more likely to believe he was related to him.

"I didn't know Dr. Hellburn had a nephew," the woman smirked maliciously. "Shall we go find him just to make sure you're who you say you are?"

"Sure, that'd be fine, although Harcourt was very angry at Mack and Haskell for disobeying his orders, and I'd hate to think how he'd react to someone questioning his nephew. I wouldn't want you to get in trouble. You know how he can be sometimes." Claude tried to sound like he really cared about her and sympathized with anyone who had to work for Dr. Hellburn.

The woman's tone changed, and her voice sounded fearful as she glanced from side to side. "Well, that's true, of course. I wouldn't want Dr. Hellburn to get angry. Not at all. . . . Carry on, then, Jason." She scurried down the hall toward the staircase and disappeared. Claude ran back to the truck with the rat.

Medea, Analena, and Claude lay flat on the bed of the truck, holding the dogs in their arms as José covered them all with the drop cloth. They whispered soothing words and begged the dogs to stay quiet when they passed the gate.

As they approached the gate, the guard stopped the truck. "Wait up," he said, putting his hand on the hood. "Mack and Haskell didn't seem to know who you were."

Peering into the back, he continued, "Hey, I thought you were dropping off dogs. What's in the back of your truck under those drop cloths? I think I'd better get Dr. Hellburn out here."

"Ah, man, I don't have time for this!" José screamed. "Those are cages for more dogs! And I'm getting paid by the dog, not by the hour." He stared into the guard's eyes with what he hoped was a dangerous and insane look.

"I *mean* it, man. Get out of my way *right now*. RIGHT NOW! Or you're gonna be real sorry. REAL SORRY!"

"All right, all right. Calm down. Go ahead. But I better not get in trouble because of you."

José sped off, exhaling a huge sigh of relief. It wasn't until they were a good ten miles past the Hellburn Research Institute, and on the highway home, that all of their hearts stopped pounding in their chests and they could breathe freely again.

Chapter 13

After the shock of what they'd done had begun to wear off, they realized that their work was far from over. They had a truck filled with dogs who needed to get back to their homes. They also had a homeless rat. They drove to José and Analena's apartment to figure out what to do next, with Claude holding Brady in his arms the whole way.

They brought the dogs up to the apartment, and Medea said, "We need to bring the dogs to the police. And we need to get them the video footage so that they can arrest Dr. Hellburn, Mack, and Haskell. The only thing is, I don't want the police to know who I am."

"That makes two of us," agreed Claude.

"What's up with that?" José asked. "We're heroes! Why shouldn't we get the credit?"

Claude and Medea exchanged glances.

"It's complicated, José. Trust me, it's not worth it. The important thing is that the dogs get home safely, and the Hellburn Research Institute is shut down," Medea answered, and then added, "And people need to know about what happens to animals in some testing laboratories."

Claude thought about what else they should do other than take the dogs to the police. He tried to remember what people did when they wanted something on the news, and he recalled all the press releases he'd heard about at his dad's news station when he went to visit him at work.

"We have to send a press release, too," Claude said.

"What's a press release?" asked José.

"Oh, it's news that people send to the media. My dad gets them all the time." Claude had slipped. He hadn't meant to mention his dad.

"Why? What does your dad do?"

"Oh, um, he's a reporter," Claude answered, hoping they wouldn't ask any more questions. Medea gave him a long stare, but said nothing.

"So, how do you do that?" José wanted to know.

"Well, we write up what happened. But press releases usually come from people who identify themselves and provide their contact information. They're not supposed to be anonymous."

"We need to have an identity then," Medea said in a very matter-of-fact manner. "Any ideas?"

Analena, who had been very quiet throughout the whole rescue, began to speak. "I think we have done something very beautiful, very good. I was scared, but I felt powerful, too, like a revolutionary righting a wrong and . . . "

Remembering that unusual word that Ms. Rattlebee had used the week before, Medea interrupted her. "I think we are like revolutionaries, Analena, but with the goal of solving problems and making a difference. I think that makes us solutionaries!"

"Solutionaries," Analena repeated the word. "I like that. I think you've found our name, Medea. We could call ourselves the Solutionary Squad."

José nodded. "I like it, too."

"Me too," Claude added, "but it sure makes us sound more powerful than we are."

"Just wait, Claude. Just wait and see how far we go." Medea's eyes sparkled as she spoke.

Maybe because they were all tired and still in a bit of shock, they didn't question whether or not what they had embarked upon was a reasonable thing for a group of kids and one man in his twenties. They all seemed to accept that they were now members of a group called the Solutionary Squad, and while they didn't yet know all that it would entail to be solutionaries, they each believed they were on the right path.

José spoke up. "Okay guys, we have work to do. I'll download the video footage and put it on a flash drive. Claude, you write that press release. You should also write up exactly what happened for the police. We'll bring the dogs and all the information to the police station. Then, we'll send the press release and the link to the video to the media. Okay?"

Everyone stared at José. His plan was perfect. They went to work.

First, they wrote up a detailed account for the police, describing everything that happened and what Claude saw and heard. In big capital letters, Claude wrote a special note about Brady and the arsenic test and said that Brady should be taken to a veterinarian immediately. Then, with Medea and Analena's help, Claude, who had seen press releases and knew something about how they were supposed to be written, started writing the press release. It took a while to get it just right. Medea wanted to make sure to say something about the Solutionary Squad's mission.

"They should know we'll be back. We have a lot more work to do after this."

Claude was too exhausted to argue, although in the back of his mind he wondered what he was committing himself to. They all agreed that they should leave out the part about the rat, since they suspected that the rat might not have been stolen and Dr. Hellburn might not be breaking any laws by experimenting on her. Here's what they finally wrote:

FOR IMMEDIATE RELEASE
Solutionary Squad Saves Stolen Dogs from Hellburn Research Institute

Members of a group called the Solutionary Squad saved seven stolen dogs from the Hellburn Research Institute in New Jersey. Observing two men trying to steal a dog from in front of Bloomingdale's on 59th and Lexington in Manhattan, a member of the Solutionary Squad hid in the men's van, which was full of dogs in cages, and videotaped their conversation. They learned that the stolen dogs were headed to the Hellburn Research Institute, where they were to be used in experiments to protect companies from lawsuits.

One of the stolen dogs was used in an arsenic test, but members of the Solutionary Squad

ZOE WEIL   97

saved him and all the other dogs, too. The dogs have been returned to the 19th Police Precinct, where it is hoped they will be reunited with their families after receiving veterinary care.

The Solutionary Squad is a group dedicated to solving problems and helping those who need help, whether they are people or animals. They will continue to work toward a better world for everyone.

By the time they had finished the police account and the press release, José had uploaded and edited the video and downloaded it onto a flash drive. Then, they piled back into José's truck and drove to the Nineteenth Precinct. Everything went smoothly. It was one a.m., and the streets on Manhattan's Upper East Side were mostly deserted. There was an alley near the precinct where they tied the dogs to a pole. The dogs, exhausted and either still recovering from the drugs they'd been given or sick from the tests they'd undergone, stayed quiet. No one saw three children and one young man hug the dogs goodbye. Nor did anyone see a girl hang a plastic bag over the police station door knob that held a detailed written account of the rescue and a flash drive that would put away the criminals for years. And no one saw the group slip quietly away and hide under the stoop of a building, where Medea made the most important phone call of her young life.

"Nineteenth Precinct," answered a woman at the police station.

"Hi. I have a crime to report. You'll find a description of the crime and a video on a flash drive with all the evidence you should need to get the criminals. It's in a bag just outside the door to the precinct. You'll also find seven rescued dogs in the alley next to your station. Thanks! Bye!"

Medea hung up quickly, and they crouched down as two police officers opened the precinct door and discovered the bag. Then, they saw them walk over to the alley and retrieve the dogs. The dogs looked up hopefully at the police officers, as if they knew they were finally going home.

After returning to José and Analena's, José created an email address for the Solutionary Squad. Using this address, they emailed the press release and the link to the video to *The New York Times*, *The Wall Street Journal*, *New York Daily News*, *New York Post*, and *The Record*, as well as to all the local TV news stations.

After they were done and ready to sleep for a couple of hours, they noticed the rat, still crammed in her plastic cage. In the rush to get the dogs to the police, they'd forgotten all about her.

Claude opened the box and gently stroked the rat's back. The rat looked up at Claude with her bright red eyes and sniffed the air.

"What are we going to do with her?" he asked no one in particular. "I'd bring her home, but it would be hard to explain where I got her."

"Same with me," Medea added, and then looked pointedly at José.

"You're kidding, right? You want us to keep her? She's a rat!"

"But she's a nice rat," Claude said beseechingly. "I'll help care for her. I'll come over to clean out her cage, and I'll pick up her rat chow." Even as Claude said this, he couldn't quite believe that these words were coming out of his mouth, but he also couldn't come up with a good reason why a rat was less worthy of kind treatment than a dog.

"Oh, all right," José said, caving. "But you better really show up to help, Claude. And we get to name her. Hey, Analena, what do you want to call her?"

Analena was quiet for a minute looking at the rat, who was still sniffing Claude's hand. She reached over to pet her back. Her fur was surprisingly soft, not coarse the way she thought it would be. The rat turned her head toward Analena and looked up at her, whiskers twitching.

"Let's call her Sol."

"Why Sol?" Claude asked.

"Well, it's short for solutionary, and it means 'sun' in Spanish. We are bringing light, and this rat is our shining example of the good we are doing. It just seems right for her, don't you think?"

Sol it was. José got a bigger box to put her in until they could get a proper cage and gave her some water and crackers. Claude and Analena petted her some more, which Sol seemed to like. Then, exhausted, they all went to bed.

Chapter 14

The next morning when they awoke, none of them was sure that they hadn't just dreamed the whole crazy story up. But there was Sol, curled up in her box.

Claude and Medea said goodbye to Analena and José and went outside. It was a beautiful fall day. They walked to school, and Claude suggested they could separate a couple of blocks before they got there so no one would see them arrive together. Medea was quiet for a minute before saying that she didn't want to hide their friendship anymore. Claude smiled. He was relieved not to have to carry that particular secret any longer.

Then, they were both quiet. Finally, Claude broke the silence. "We did something, Medea."

"We sure did, Claude. I wonder what Ms. Rattlebee would think?"

"I think she'd think it was pretty cool," Claude answered.

"I think she'd say it's just the beginning, although I'm not sure she'd want us risking our lives in our efforts to make a difference," Medea said, staring into Claude's eyes.

Claude smiled at her. Her eyes were so intense, deep and dark like inkwells. He was glad to have found a real friend. He was proud of what they'd done, although he also worried that they might not be so lucky next time.

Just then, they were startled, and then pleased, to see a tiny woman wearing a skirt made from neckties walking toward them.

"Well hello, dears!" Ms. Rattlebee exclaimed as she looked up at them.

"Hi, Ms. Rattlebee! What are you doing here?" Medea replied.

"Oh, I'm just out for a walk on this lovely day. How nice to see you two walking together." Ms. Rattlebee had a knowing smile on her face, as if she had expected to run into the two of them.

Claude and Medea looked at each other and then back at Ms. Rattlebee.

"Ms. Rattlebee," Medea began, not sure exactly what she wanted to say, but wanting to take advantage of this auspicious moment, "your classes were great. They had a big impact on us. We're glad you left your phone number, because we want to call you sometime." Claude just stared at Medea as she said this. *Medea is so awesome*, he thought.

"Well, I'm so glad, dear Medea. I would love to hear from you. Anything I can do to help, you just call me. You two are on the right track, but just remember to be wise and careful. See you soon, then!" And off she went, the multicolored ties swaying as she walked away.

"Didn't it seem like she knew something, Medea? Something about us?"

"You may be right, Claude. I think there's a lot more to Ms. Rattlebee than we know."

After an interminably long day, school was finally over and Claude rushed home. Rooper was there to greet him. He hugged his dog hard and felt his eyes get watery and his throat constrict. Imagining Rooper in the testing lab at the Hellburn Research Institute was too awful to bear. Rooper licked Claude's face and eyelids reassuringly. Claude and Medea had decided not to walk Rooper together after school because they were both exhausted and had homework to do, but Claude planned to walk Rooper by himself, for as long as his dog wanted.

They wandered all over the park. Some of the leaves on the trees were beginning to change, and the air was fresh and cool. Claude thought about how much his life had changed in such a short time. "Who would've thought . . . ?" he said to himself and smiled.

When he got back home, he went to his room to do his homework and practice violin. Sophie prepared pasta primavera for him. He thanked her for remembering his new diet and ate his dinner quietly. Eventually, his dad got home and came to Claude's room.

"Hi, Claude."

"Hey, Dad. Anything new in the world?"

"As a matter of fact, yes. Take a look at this." Farnsworth handed Claude his phone, which was opened to an article in *The New York Times*.

"Amazing story. Some people calling themselves the Solutionary Squad solved those dognappings we were talking about."

With trembling hands, Claude picked up his dad's phone and started reading.

SOLUTIONARY SQUAD SAVES DOGS, PUTS RESEARCH INSTITUTE IN DOGHOUSE

By Trillium Reed

A group calling themselves the Solutionary Squad solved the recent Manhattan dog thefts and saved seven stolen dogs from the Hellburn Research Institute in Bergen County, New Jersey. While they are not taking any personal credit for their efforts, their group vows to help anyone who needs it, "whether they are people or animals."

Members of the Solutionary Squad videotaped the men who stole the dogs and then captured footage of conditions inside the Institute. They caught Dr. Harcourt Hellburn, the director of the Hellburn Institute (HRI), mistreating one of the dogs used in an arsenic test. They managed to free the dogs without getting caught themselves.

Preliminary information suggests that Harcourt Hellburn not only paid personnel to steal dogs for his experiments, but may have also conducted illegal, non-scientific, profit-driven studies on animals solely to protect his clients from lawsuits.

Members of the Solutionary Squad brought the dogs to the 19th Precinct, and the animals are currently being reunited with their families. The dogs used in the experiments are receiving treatment, and Dr. Saveur from the Saveur Animal Hospital expects them to make a full recovery. Matilda Newhouse, guardian of Brady, a dog used in an arsenic test, had this to say: "The people who saved my little Brady are true angels. I'm forever grateful."

Dr. Hellburn and his associates have been arrested, and HRI has been shut down pending a complete investigation into dog theft, fraud, and criminal animal cruelty. The police chief in Bergen County, NJ, has also said that they will be opening a department to ascertain whether similar cruelty and fraud may be occurring in other New Jersey laboratories that use animals in research.

It's likely that we haven't seen the last of the Solutionary Squad, but Detective Bloodworth of the 19th Precinct says that while the members of the Solutionary Squad may be trying to do good deeds, they should leave police work to the police. He vows to find out who is involved and put a stop to what he terms "their foolhardy shenanigans."

"What do you think of this story, Dad?" Claude asked. "I mean, what do you think of those people called the Solutionary Squad?"

"They're courageous, Claude, but foolish. If they had gotten caught, who knows what would have happened to them. Anyone who would steal dogs and conduct experiments on them is quite dangerous in my book. Still, you've got to be impressed with something like this. Now, time to get ready for bed, kiddo."

Farnsworth left the room, and Marisa came in to check on Claude. While he was brushing his teeth, Marisa read the article on her phone, and as Claude walked back in, she looked at him strangely.

"What's wrong, Marisa?"

She stared at him intently. "That's quite an article, Claude. You must be happy to know that the dog you met has been rescued."

"Oh yeah, definitely," Claude replied nervously but with a pleased look on his face.

"I imagine you're relieved, too."

"Absolutely. A big relief. Well, good night, Marisa."

"Good night, Claude." She had a quizzical expression on her face as she closed the door behind her.

As Claude lay in bed with Rooper curled up next to him, he thought about Gandhi's quote and realized that he felt pretty good about his life's message. And as he drifted off to sleep, he wondered about the ways in which he would continue to make his life the message he wanted it to be in the months and years ahead.

A FINAL WORD

Not everyone knows how to have such a powerful impact on kids as Ms. Rattlebee. The Institute for Humane Education (IHE) offers programs and resources so that people who want to make a difference in the world can be inspiring educators like she is. We hope that more and more teachers will offer classes like Flora Rattlebee, whether or not they are very short.

The Institute for Humane Education also helps people of all ages become solutionaries. To be clear, we do not think kids should endanger themselves or break the law. Let's leave that to fictional children like Claude, Medea, and their friends in the Solutionary Squad.

Zoe Weil, President
Institute for Humane Education
www.HumaneEducation.org

About the Author

 **Zoe Weil** is the cofounder and president of the Institute for Humane Education (IHE) and the author of seven books, including Amazon #1 Best Seller in the Philosophy and Social Aspects of Education, *The World Becomes What We Teach*, and Nautilus silver medal winner *Most Good, Least Harm*. Zoe was named one of *Maine Magazine*'s fifty independent leaders transforming their communities and the state and is the recipient of the Women in Environmental Leadership award. She was also a subject of the *Americans Who Tell the Truth* portrait series. She is a frequent keynote speaker at educational and changemaking conferences and has given six TEDx talks. Zoe created the first graduate programs in humane education, offered through an affiliation with Antioch University. After decades of teaching young people about how to solve problems in our communities and world and create a future where all people, animals, and nature can thrive, she decided to write fiction for tweens. Moonbeam Gold Medal winner for juvenile fiction, *Claude & Medea*, is the result. Her website is HumaneEducation.org

About the Publisher

Lantern Publishing & Media was founded in 2020 to follow and expand on the legacy of Lantern Books—a publishing company started in 1999 on the principles of living with a greater depth and commitment to the preservation of the natural world. Like its predecessor, Lantern Publishing & Media produces books on animal advocacy, veganism, religion, social justice, humane education, psychology, family therapy, and recovery. Lantern is dedicated to printing in the United States on recycled paper and saving resources in our day-to-day operations. Our titles are also available as ebooks and audiobooks.

To catch up on Lantern's publishing program, visit us at www.lanternpm.org.

 facebook.com/lanternpm
instagram.com/lanternpm
twitter.com/lanternpm